They stood there for a heartbeat that felt like a lifetime, staring at each other

When was the last time he'd impulsively kissed a woman? This had been thoroughly spontaneous, and he was glad. If he'd stopped to think first, he might not have done it.

Adam cleared his throat. "I'll round up my kids."

Brenna nodded, bemused.

Neither of them said anything else, but when he got to the back door, he couldn't resist looking over his shoulder at her. She remained in the same spot, motionless. Except that she'd pressed her fingers to her lips.

As he stepped through the door, a whisper of sound followed him.

He thought it might have been *wow*.

Dear Reader,

I grew up surrounded by a lot of happy chaos—relatives visiting, friends in and out of the house and pets underfoot. (At one point we owned three dogs, two cats and a ferret, all of whom played together.) An adult now with kids of my own, I am definitely carrying on the chaotic tradition.

In *Mistletoe Mommy* I bring that tradition to Mistletoe, Georgia. Brenna Pierce is a pet sitter who thinks the biggest complication in her life is a broken-down car—until Dr. Adam Varner and his three children roll into town for summer vacation! Trying to get her self-owned business up and running, Brenna doesn't have time for romance. And Adam certainly isn't looking for a relationship. He already has his hands full trying to bond with a teenage son, surly "tween" daughter and a little girl obsessed with getting a cat for her fifth birthday. Yet, amid the chaos of animals and kids, Brenna and Adam discover love and something that feels remarkably like family.

This is my third book in the 4 SEASONS IN MISTLETOE miniseries, and I hope you enjoy reading them as much as I've loved writing them! Watch for the series conclusion, *Mistletoe Hero*, in October 2009.

Wishing you only the happiest chaos,

Tanya

Mistletoe Mommy
TANYA MICHAELS

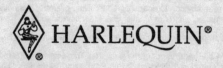

HARLEQUIN®

TORONTO • NEW YORK • LONDON
AMSTERDAM • PARIS • SYDNEY • HAMBURG
STOCKHOLM • ATHENS • TOKYO • MILAN • MADRID
PRAGUE • WARSAW • BUDAPEST • AUCKLAND

Recycling programs
for this product may
not exist in your area.

ISBN-13: 978-0-373-75274-4

MISTLETOE MOMMY

Copyright © 2009 by Tanya Michna.

ABOUT THE AUTHOR

Tanya Michaels began telling stories almost as soon as she could talk...and started stealing her mom's Harlequin romances less than a decade later. In 2003 Tanya was thrilled to have her first book, a romantic comedy, published by Harlequin Books. Since then, Tanya has sold nearly twenty books and is a two-time recipient of the Booksellers' Best Award as well as a finalist for the Holt Medallion, National Readers' Choice Award and Romance Writers of America's prestigious RITA® Award. Tanya lives in Georgia with her husband, two preschoolers and an unpredictable cat, but you can visit Tanya online at www.tanyamichaels.com.

Books by Tanya Michaels

*4 Seasons in Mistletoe

This book is dedicated to the caring and
hardworking ladies of
Koala T. Care Pet Sitting and Dog Walking.

Chapter One

The day Brenna Pierce was having would be enough to drive any woman crazy. Which, in Brenna's case, would actually be an improvement, because at least she would be driving *somewhere*.

Instead, she paced alongside a curvy stretch of blacktop in the pounding late-June heat. Her stepfather had raised her to believe that swearing was vulgar, but now, sweaty and exasperated, Brenna mentally chanted a stream of four-letter words, running them together in an all-purpose Über-Curse. Coincidentally, *loan* was a four-letter word—and something she might have to apply for soon.

She'd been praying her ancient hatchback would make it through this summer, but the faded green car appeared to be on its last legs. Er, tires.

Her cell phone wasn't currently working, either. No bars here. Maybe she'd unintentionally discovered Mistletoe, Georgia's answer to the Bermuda Triangle, a magnolia-lined stretch of asphalt where all things mechanical sputtered and died. Investigating scientists could name it the Brenna Straightaway.

To find a patch with better reception, she'd climbed out of the car. Her pacing hadn't netted any results yet, but she couldn't cover more than a few yards without taking along the vehicle's occupant, Lady Evelyn. Wiping damp strands of coppery hair away from her face, Brenna glanced through the open window. Lady Evelyn, a Yorkshire terrier, sat in the back seat wearing her safety restraint harness as imperiously as though it were crown jewels. The Yorkie glared, unamused by first the lack of air-conditioning—fixing the A/C would cost more than the car was worth—and now the unscheduled stop.

At least Brenna had managed to almost coast to the shoulder. Though the vehicle wasn't as out of the way as she would have liked, it also wasn't in the middle of the road.

Reaching inside, she patted her canine companion on the head. "What do you say, Evelyn? Wanna get out and help me push?"

Beneath the pink bow holding up silky hair, the dog's dark eyes seemed incredulous. *Surely you jest. I'm a prizewinning purebred. I have ribbons. I don't do manual labor.*

Hearing doggie voices in her head couldn't possibly be a good sign. *I have got to get out of the heat.* Even more importantly, Brenna had to reach Patch by three-thirty. Four o'clock at the latest.

Brenna grabbed the leash from the front seat. "Come on," she said, unfastening Lady Evelyn's safety harness. "Let's go for a walk."

If they were lucky, she'd get cell reception just up the road and reach someone who could drop everything to come give them a ride. Preferably someone with air-conditioning. They hadn't gone far when a car came barreling over the hill. Brenna waved her arm.

As she squinted against the sunlight, she made out the people inside the oncoming vehicle: Rachel and David Waide. For a minute she didn't think they were going to stop—odd, since the popular Mistletoe couple could usually be counted on to help anyone—but then David swerved to a haphazard halt just past her parked lemon. She scooped up Lady Evelyn and jogged toward the Waides.

David rolled down the window, his handsome face surprisingly pale in spite of a summer tan. "Brenna! Are you okay? We're just on our way to take Dr. McDermott to the hospital."

From the passenger seat, his very pregnant wife leaned over with a grin. "He means we're on our way to *meet* Dr. McDermott. My water— Oh!"

David swung back to Rachel. "I lost track of how far apart they are. I'm supposed to be keeping track!"

"Doesn't matter," Rachel gasped. "Just *drive*."

He turned to Brenna. "If you need a lift, hop in, but we have to go straight to the hospital. Rach is in labor!"

Brenna nodded, hiding a smile. "I got that. You two

run along." They obviously didn't have time to take her to Patch and were going in the opposite direction from where she needed to be.

David eased off the brake, the car beginning to roll as he asked, "What about you?"

Maybe he could call someone for her on his way? The Waide family owned a supply store not too far from here. Perhaps one of his siblings, Arianne or Tanner, could come get her. She hadn't been planning to call them, but it would be easiest for David to dial a number he already had programmed into his phone.

"Could you—" She broke off at the sound of another automobile approaching. "Never mind. You take care of your wife. I'll get help from the next Good Samaritan."

Not waiting to be told twice, David pulled away.

"Good luck," Brenna called after them. Then she focused on the brown SUV coming into view, gesturing with her free hand.

The car slowed and veered off the road. She saw two males in the front—one considerably younger than the other—and tops of heads that indicated shorter passengers in the back. She recognized neither the vehicle nor the inhabitants.

Still carrying the Yorkshire terrier, hardly an armful at five and a half pounds, Brenna neared the driver's side. A dark-haired man rolled down his window. She'd never passed him in town; he was someone she would have remembered. His face was perhaps the most geometrically perfect she'd ever seen—symmetrical features, strong jaw, straight nose, well-defined cheekbones and eyes so dark their color was unfathomable. On a blindingly bright day like this one, they made her think of cool, shaded pools.

Brenna gave a quick shake of her head, such poetic thoughts unlike her. *Definitely been in the sun too long.*

"Hi," she said. "I'm Brenna Pierce. You're not from Mistletoe, are you?"

"No, just vacationing here." His deep voice was a touch rueful.

An adolescent female from the back seat piped up with, "You mean we've finally made it to Mistletoe? It feels like we've been driving around for days," she added on a whine.

The boy, who shared the driver's features but in a blocky, awkward, not-yet-grown-into way, whirled around. "Maybe if you *girls* didn't have to stop every five minutes, Dad could have paid better attention to the map."

"Well, if *boys* weren't too stubborn to admit when they're lost—"

An excited, high-pitched voice interrupted. "Doggie! Daddy, can I pet the doggie?"

As three children chorused various questions and complaints, the man driving the SUV asked Brenna, "So did you need some help, ma'am?"

"As a matter of fact, yes." Wincing as the noise level from inside the SUV escalated, she found herself thinking, *But who's gonna help* you?

Chapter Two

Dr. Adam Varner squelched the urge to throw himself out of his car and beg for mercy from the stranger. Even though he'd assured Sara that he'd have no trouble with the kids—*I'm their father, for pity's sake, I spend nearly every day in an operating room, how hard can this be?*—he'd realized in the last hundred miles that parenting was far more difficult than he remembered.

What the heck had happened to Morgan, the apple-cheeked infant? Eliza, aka Daddy's Girl? Or Geoff, the doting son who'd wanted to be just like his father? Now they were a soon-to-be kindergartener, a sullen preteen and a teen obsessed with cars and girls. Admittedly those were probably normal interests for a fifteen-year-old, but Adam had to keep reminding himself that the kid was no longer content with a skateboard-scooter.

Amid Morgan's inquiries of "are we almost there?" and Geoff's insistence that he was hungry again, even though he'd had lunch a couple of hours ago *and* wiped out the stash of snacks inside the SUV, Adam had been switching through satellite radio stations and suggesting car games in a desperate search for a distraction. He certainly hadn't expected roadside diversion in the form of a tall redhead and her rag mop of a dog.

Adam had grown up with a German shepherd and a black Lab. The piece of fluff Brenna Pierce held looked like it would lose a street fight to a gerbil. Even though he knew nothing about her, somehow the immaculately groomed lapdog looked all wrong for her. Brenna's tan suggested lots of outdoor activity, as did her footgear— instead of strappy summer sandals, she wore a pair of blue-and-silver hiking shoes. She needed a sturdy dog that could keep up with her. And if she was single, maybe something big enough to growl at intruders.

Was she single? he wondered absently.

He opened his door, unfastening his seat belt with the other hand. "I take it that's your car?"

She shot the green hatchback a glare of pure loathing. "Yeah, it's mine."

"Did it overheat?" He hazarded a guess, reasoning that even an igloo could overheat in weather like this. The air around them was sticky, and he wouldn't have been surprised to see the tar-based road beneath their feet come to a boil.

"The gauge didn't show any signs of overheating, but who knows? Gauge could be busted. Just about everything else is."

Already unbuckling his own seat belt, Geoff asked, "Can I come take a look, too?"

As much time as the teen spent reading car magazines these days, he probably knew more about automotive mechanics than his father. Adam was used to working with his hands, but in surgery not in garages. "Sure. But stay off to the side of the road. Your mother would kill me if you wandered into traffic on my watch."

This elicited a snort from Eliza, a formerly delightful child who seemed to have developed a personality disorder moments after blowing out the twelve candles on her last birthday cake. "Traffic? We're in the backwoods of nowhere. They probably only get one car a day on this road."

Brenna cocked her head to the side, smiling at his daughter through the open door. "Actually, someone passed by less than five minutes ago."

At an apparent loss for a response, Eliza merely twisted a strand of her long hair and looked away. It was such a change from the constant sniping that Adam wanted to cheer. Instead, he asked Brenna, "The people ahead of us didn't stop for you?" That didn't bode well for the friendly small town he'd been promised in the tourism literature.

"They paused briefly, but were on the way to the county hospital. The passenger was in labor," she explained, stepping aside to let Geoff pass, "so I told them I'd try to flag down the next car. I heard you coming by then and was hoping you'd be someone I knew. But—" She stopped, checking her watch. The leather band was covered with paw-print cutouts. Her hair, styled in a short, elegant bob, was tucked behind her ears, revealing matching silver paw-print studs.

"Problem?" Adam asked as she scowled.

"Time crunch. Would I sound too melodramatic if I said it was a life-or-death situation?"

"That's my specialty," he assured her wryly. Had he even introduced himself? Being trapped in the SUV with the kids had robbed him of his adult people skills. "I'm Dr. Adam Varner, cardiac surgeon from Knoxville. My children and I are staying in Mistletoe until just after July fourth."

"At least two and a half weeks? Wish I could get my clients to go away for that long," she murmured, more to herself than him. "Then I could replace the lemon."

"Clients?"

"I'm a local pet-sitter, owner of More than Puppy Love. I take care of other people's animals. Like Lady Evelyn here. And Patch, a diabetic cat. His owner is in Savannah on business. I have to make sure Patch gets his daily insulin shots on time."

"Someone keeps a pet even though they have to give it shots every day?" Eliza asked, climbing out from the back seat. Adam should have known that if he let one kid out, the others would follow. Just as well—they probably needed to stretch their legs. "Sounds like a lot of trouble."

"It's not ideal," Brenna said, "but most of my clients consider their pets family members. You go the extra mile for someone you love."

Though Adam couldn't see his daughter's expression behind him, he felt her accusing stare boring holes into his skull. Was she thinking of the instances he hadn't made enough time for his own loved ones? He sighed, trying to be patient. It was true that he'd been overwhelmed by the demands of residency at the hospital and hadn't been the husband and father Sara and the kids had deserved. But Sara had just remarried, happily moving on with her life, and Adam was doing his level best to reconnect with his kids. By the end of the summer, they'd see that.

I hope.

"Daddy doesn't like pets." This was from curly-haired Morgan, not her terminally ticked-off older sister.

"That's not true." He turned, defending himself in a mild tone. "I grew up with animals. I've always liked animals."

"But you wouldn't get a dog for your place," Eliza said. "Which would have been the perfect solution since we can't have one at our house!"

Our house—the house he'd bought right after Sara discovered she was pregnant with Morgan. Sara had asked him to move out just before their youngest daughter's first birthday. Watching his wife—ex-wife—marry someone else last weekend had been something of a wake-up call. An entirely new household was forming under his erstwhile roof; he was more determined than ever to make up for lost time. He never again wanted to feel as if he'd blinked and missed entire chunks of his children's lives.

"Daddy Dan's allergic to dogs," Morgan informed Brenna, creeping forward with a hand outstretched to the Yorkie.

With effort, Adam managed not to flinch at the "Daddy Dan." After all, Sara's new husband had earned the moniker. He'd been there for Eliza's dance recital when Adam's patient had encountered postsurgical complications. Adam had tried to make the most of watching her ballet solo with her on tape afterward, but she hadn't been mollified. Dan had also been there when Morgan got the chicken pox, sitting up with her at night to reapply calamine lotion and distract her from her misery. He was a good guy.

Pushing away an immature stab of resentment, Adam reminded Eliza, "I didn't want to get a dog, because it wouldn't be fair. I'm not home enough to take care of it and give it the companionship it deserves."

"Right. You're always at the hospital," his daughter agreed. She flounced off to join her brother by Brenna's car, not giving him much chance to respond.

He shot an embarrassed look at Brenna. Unaware of his past missteps with his daughter and the latitude he was trying to give her now, Brenna must think Eliza was a demon child and that he was the world's most ineffectual parent. The redhead wasn't looking at him, however.

Instead, she busied herself with showing Morgan how "Lady Evelyn" liked to be petted. Not for a minute did he believe Brenna had missed the tense exchange, but he was grateful she was pretending not to notice.

"I have my cell phone in the SUV," he told her. "We can call someone for you. Or we can give you a ride, if that will get you to the cat faster."

Brenna set down the dog but held on to the leash, not that the pooch seemed motivated to escape Morgan's adoration. "We can try your phone, but reception in this particular spot is lousy. I would have called someone by now if I could get a signal. And I really *do* need to reach Patch."

"We're happy to take you," he reiterated.

She bit her lip. "Well, I wouldn't normally…"

Come to think of it, was he setting a terrible example picking up a stranger? He'd make sure the kids understood later that this was a rare exception. In her khaki shorts and navy-striped tank top, both of which revealed long, well-toned limbs, he couldn't imagine where Brenna would conceal any weapons. Since he outweighed her by probably forty or fifty pounds, he was confident he could take her physically—a random thought that somehow got all turned around in his mind and heightened his awareness of the golden expanse of dewy skin.

Luckily Brenna, who was looking around at his kids, was oblivious.

She turned to him with the beginnings of a smile. "You don't exactly seem like an escaped convict."

He pulled his wallet from his jeans pocket and handed her his Tennessee driver's license. "I'm an upstanding citizen, I swear. The only thing scary about me is my association with—" he affected a shudder "—*teenagers*. They're not for the faint of heart."

She laughed, a warm, husky sound. Pleasure tightened inside him, and he reminded himself that a responsible single father didn't get lust-stricken on the side of a dusty road over a total stranger with his three kids standing right there. His sole purpose in Mistletoe was to focus on rebuilding his relationships with his children. He had only a few weeks to make up for the past few years. There was no room for distractions.

Brenna pulled a business card out of her pocket and handed it back with his license. "I once helped take care of a ball python, so I should be able to brave teenagers."

"It's settled, then," Adam said. "We'll take you to give Patch his injection and to figure out what to do about your car once the medical crisis has passed."

She hesitated only a heartbeat before nodding. "Let me grab Lady E's bag out of my car and make sure the doors are unlocked. With any luck, some enterprising thief will figure out a way to get it running and steal it."

BRENNA WAS ACCUSTOMED to odd "herds." She'd once worked for a family who owned a domesticated pig, two hermit crabs and a ferret. And she was no stranger to unusual human clans, having been raised by a man with no biological ties to her and a woman who would have been well within her right to resent the heck out of her presence. So despite Dr. Adam Varner's alternately mortified and apologetic glances during their

drive into Mistletoe town proper, she was mostly un-
daunted by his children's antics.

The littlest Varner, with her mop of unruly honey-
gold curls and light eyes, looked the least like her
father and was also the least inhibited. Brenna would
have expected such a small child to be shy, but Morgan
chattered constantly. She was the one who volunteered
that they were on "vay-cay-tion," pronouncing the
word with emphatic concentration, "because Mama
and Daddy Dan wanted alone time to kiss. Last week
I saw Geoff kissing his girlfriend on our couch!"

"Mor*gan!*" Her brother's voice cracked on the second syllable. He leaned forward, poking his head between the front seats. "Please excuse my sister. She's
too young to understand adult matters."

Brenna managed to keep a straight face as she
nodded, but his sister Eliza didn't bother hiding her
derisive snort.

"Adult?" She chortled. "You just turned fifteen. You
can't even get a driver's license until your next birthday."

"I have my learner's permit," he said stiffly, "and
I'm a lot more—"

"Kids," Adam interjected warningly, "can't we—"

"—grown up than *you,*" Geoff finished. "You cry half
the time for no reason at all. Even Morgan doesn't—"

"That's *enough,*" Adam said, this time hitting the
palm of his hand on the steering wheel for emphasis.
"I don't want to hear another word for the rest of the
ride. Does everyone understand?"

Eliza, who was either fearless or harbored a death wish, muttered, "Are we allowed to answer that?"

Despite herself, Brenna was fascinated by the ill-mannered girl. Brenna herself had possessed more reason for anger than most adolescents, yet she'd remained unnaturally well behaved. It had taken her years to shake the terror that her stepfather and his new wife—who was actually his *old* wife, long story—might decide they didn't want her.

After all, Brenna's own mother hadn't kept her, not only leaving her husband, Fred Pierce, but leaving Brenna behind in Mistletoe. Brenna hadn't known whether to feel betrayed or relieved.

"Sorry about all this," Adam said to Brenna.

"No worries. You're doing me the favor," she reminded him.

He jerked his head back, indicating the three now-quiet passengers behind them. "I would say they fight like cats and dogs, but cats and dogs probably get along better."

Her lips twitched as she thought of her own two pets, a wickedly smart border-collie mix and a cat who thought she was a dog. They were the best of friends.

"Their mother, Sara, assures me sibling rivalry is natural, so I'll take her word for it. I'm an only child myself," Adam told her, no trace of conflict in his voice when he mentioned the ex who'd remarried. "You have any brothers or sisters?"

"A younger stepbrother, but we never fought." She

said it automatically, regretting that she'd added it. It would only make Adam feel more conscious of his *own* brood, which was a lousy way to repay him for taking the time to help her.

To fill the embarrassed silence, she gave directions and commentary on the town. "Up here at the corner, we'll turn left to get to Patch's house. If you make a right on that same road, you can follow the signs to Kerrigan Farms. It's a great place. They have a Fourth of July barbecue and blueberry picking all year round, as well as hayrides. We're also just a couple of blocks from the Dixieland Diner. They have *phenomenal* food."

"Food," Geoff moaned, his apparent starvation prompting him to break the not-a-word edict.

Brenna impulsively turned to Adam. "After I take care of Patch and drop Lady E at home, would you let me buy you an early dinner?" He was going out of his way to help her, and being indebted to anyone else left her squirmy and anxious. "Please? It's the least I can do for you guys."

Geoff let out a whoop of delight, which his father quickly overruled.

"I can't let you pay for the four of us," Adam objected. "Especially since one of us, who shall remain nameless, eats like a horse."

"But…" She trailed off as common sense reasserted itself. Aside from her almost pathological need to repay him, it was probably for the best if they didn't have dinner together.

She had a ton of phone messages to catch up on this evening and invoices to type into her computer. This was supposed to be the summer when she worked as many long hours as humanly possible so that she was solvent by fall, when schools were back in session and her customers' travel plans slowed down. Buying dinner for large families she didn't know was not in her meager budget.

"Wait," she said, suddenly realizing where they were, "that's Martine Street! We're supposed to hook a left here."

He immediately obliged.

"Thanks. Sorry about the short notice." She was already fishing through the lockbox she'd retrieved from her car for the key to the client's house. "Patch lives in the big blue two-story at the bottom of the hill. I promise not to take too long." Next stop, Lady Evelyn's house. The Yorkie's owners would be back from Florida tonight. They hadn't wanted the pampered dog to miss her standing appointment at the groomer, so Brenna had taken her.

Adam parked the SUV at the curb. "Does your offer of dinner with us hold even if I don't let you pay? We'd love the chance to hear more about the town, wouldn't we, kids?"

"Yes!" Geoff agreed vehemently.

Brenna got the impression that Adam's son would agree to anything that led to getting fed. She hesitated, thinking of everything she needed to get done at her home office. Then again, how could she refuse when dinner had been her idea in the first place?

"I'll let you pick up the tip," Adam said, adding under his voice, "I'm not sure I'm ready to be left alone with these three again. I don't know what I'm doing."

She laughed. "All right," she agreed as she climbed out of the car.

Even though he'd had a joking tone, she believed him when he said he wasn't ready to be alone with the kids. Though he was an intelligent, funny man—and a *surgeon,* for pity's sake, which indicated a high level of capability—he did seem a bit awkward with his own children. Parenting just didn't come naturally to some.

Brenna knew that better than anyone.

Chapter Three

Bracing himself, Adam prepared to lay down the law if the kids resumed their bickering now that Brenna had disappeared into the blue house. But Morgan seemed content telling Lady Evelyn how cute she was, and Eliza had her eyes closed and gave every appearance of napping. Geoff, in contrast, was practically vibrating with excitement.

"Way to go, Dad! She's a babe."

Adam choked. "Geoffrey, that's not an appropriate way for you to discuss Ms. Pierce."

"Oh, but—" his son looked more bemused than chastised "—didn't you see her?"

What was more disturbing? That the kid who'd thought girls were gross a few years ago was now scoping out older women, or that Adam wholeheartedly agreed with the fifteen-year-old's assessment?

"I saw her. And she is attractive," he admitted in a vast understatement. "You need to show more respect, though."

"Sorry," Geoff mumbled. "I just wanted to be, you know, supportive. Do you *ever* date?"

Rarely. His job occupied most of his waking hours, and more than once he'd sat up in bed realizing he'd been going through a case or procedure in his sleep.

"Are we gonna have two mommies like we have two daddies?" Morgan asked.

"What?" Adam spun in his seat so that he could better face his children. "No, pumpkin. Of course not. I only met Ms. Pierce a few minutes ago."

"But Geoff said you might date. Mama and Daddy Dan used to date and now they're married." She concluded her observation with a nod, agreeing with her own logic.

"That's true, but—"

"If we get more parents, do we get more presents?" Morgan wanted to know.

She was turning five at the end of next week, so birthday presents were uppermost in her mind. Sara and Dan had hosted an early party for her, not wanting her big day to be eclipsed by their recent mid-June wedding. Sara had told Adam it was up to him to figure out a way to celebrate the actual day on vacation. She wouldn't even advise him what gift to get, as she had for most previous birthdays and Christmases.

"It should be from *you*," she'd insisted gently.

"How about just a hint?" he'd wheedled. She'd laughed but hadn't answered. Some of Morgan's interests were obvious, of course. She loved pink and she loved animals, but he had no idea what toys she already owned, or if certain brands of adorable puppy figurines were preferable to others.

Before Adam could repeat that no one was getting additional parents anytime soon, Eliza straightened, opening her eyes just enough to glare at him. *Naturally.*

"Dad is not here to date," she informed her siblings. "Mom promised this trip would be all about him spending time with us. *Right?*" She hurled the one-word question at Adam like a shot put.

Underneath the hostility was so much vulnerability that Adam wanted to scramble over the seat and hug her. *As if she'd let you.* This was one prickly kid. He couldn't help wondering if Sara had shielded him from this, sighing and taking care of the preteen's attitude, instead of calling to yell at him for the monster he'd created. Had she talked to the kids before he came over last Thanksgiving, admonishing them to be on their best behavior? Or had Eliza simply bottled all this up, saving it for the right target? Not having any brothers or sisters himself, he couldn't determine whether being the middle child was truly the most difficult family position, but it seemed accurate in Eliza's case.

Morgan had been so young when he and Sara split up that she didn't clearly remember a time they'd been married. Geoff had been old enough to understand how critical Adam's job was, that sometimes it really was a matter of life or death, and he'd been coming into more independent years, so he hadn't been as bothered by

Adam's absences. At least, that was the mature stance he projected; Adam had let himself buy into it because it was comforting. But Eliza… She'd fallen somewhere in between, and the divorce had wounded her badly.

"This trip is definitely about you kids," he vowed. "I've never taken this much time off work before, and—"

"We're so sorry to have messed up your schedule," she snapped.

He'd said what he had to make her feel important, not to complain about being inconvenienced. *What would Sara do?* He couldn't imagine his ex-wife allowing Eliza to be a brat. Then again, Sara had never done anything to earn such legitimate enmity. Was Adam reaping what he deserved? Regardless, this wasn't the tone he wanted to set for the rest of their stay in Mistletoe, nor was it the behavioral example he wanted to set for Morgan.

"Eliza, I have to ask you to watch your tone," he said. Her eyebrows shot up, her dark eyes firing sparks at him, but he pressed bravely forward. "I understand you're angry—"

"You don't understand me! You don't even know me!"

"I'm trying to," he said firmly.

She met his gaze, but said nothing further. Finally she looked out the window. Was it his overly hopeful imagination, or had a tiny bit of tension drained from her slim body? At least she seemed to be thinking about what he'd said, instead of firing back a rejoinder about how they were just fine without him. Small steps.

After all, no one walked into an operating room their first day of med school and performed a cardio-pulmonary bypass. There were lessons that had to be learned, techniques that had to be perfected. He didn't delude himself that he would ever be a perfect father, but surely, with practice, he could do better than *this*. Half the time she gave the hostile impression that she would take out a contract hit on him if only her allow-ance were high enough.

Figuring he'd done what he could to pacify one daughter for the moment, he turned to the other. Morgan had watched the exchange with increasingly wide eyes.

He reached between the seats, awkwardly patting her on the knee. "You okay, pumpkin?"

"Yeah." She wrinkled her nose. "Just hungry."

"We'll eat right after we take the dog home," Adam promised.

Geoff beamed at him. "I got so wigged-out the first time I asked Gina for a date that I thought I was gonna blow chow. Without even trying, you got a girl to invite you to dinner *and* she offered to pay. Awesome."

Adam pinched the bridge of his nose. *Well, at least one of my kids thinks I'm doing something right.*

As ADAM NAVIGATED the crowded parking lot outside the Dixieland Diner, Brenna dialed Quinn Keller's number. The two women had been casual acquain-tances for years, but recently they'd become closer friends. Quinn lived in a duplex, two adjoining homes that shared a front and backyard. The other half belonged to Dylan Echols, who'd surprised his widowed mother with a maltipoo puppy on Mother's Day. But he'd been thoughtful enough to first work with Brenna for a few weeks to get the dog housebroken and trained to obey basic commands. Quinn, a teacher at Whiteberry Elementary, had watched the pup's progress from her front porch and even helped with a few lessons.

As the two women got to know each other, they'd discussed Quinn working part-time for Brenna once business was more established. Brenna wanted to grow her customer base for financial reasons and job security, but even with the number of clients she already had, she was hard-pressed to handle the volume of summer and holiday visits—the same times of the year that Quinn had off from teaching—by herself. If Quinn would answer her phone now, she could even ride with Brenna on a few jobs tonight as preliminary training.

Unfortunately Brenna only reached a mechanical voice telling her to leave a message. She knew Adam would take her home if she asked but she'd already imposed and didn't want to take the Varners farther out of their way after their long day on the road. *So call Fred or Josh. No biggie.* It shouldn't be a "biggie." After all, she'd been part of their family for nearly twenty years.

But she'd been conditioned for the formative first thirteen years of her life not to get too attached, that she didn't truly belong anywhere.

Would she have overcome that neurosis if Fred, her stepfather, hadn't remarried Josh's mother, Maggie? That woman had been the true love of Fred Pierce's life, but in their first marriage they'd grown apart over time and divorced. He'd hastily rebounded with Brenna's mother, only to have her slink off in the middle of the night for parts unknown. Though Brenna had never asked, she'd often wondered if his emotional response to being abandoned had mirrored hers—equal parts betrayal and relief.

About a year later, Maggie had been diagnosed with ovarian cancer, still at an early stage. The medical crisis had shaken Fred enough that he'd started courting her again. Josh had what all children-of-divorce secretly dreamed of—his parents back together, his family a healed whole.

With Brenna as the fly in the ointment. *Awkward.*

Ancient history, she told herself. She'd risen above her unorthodox upbringing, loved the entire Pierce family; she was a productive member of society. *Whose previous boyfriend dumped you because you relate better to animals than people.*

Funny, he hadn't seemed to mind that about her when he'd hired her; her last serious boyfriend was also the town veterinarian. She'd enjoyed working in the clinic, but had always known that she wouldn't be working as his receptionist/critter referee forever. Their breakup nearly two years ago had helped motivate her to get her small business off the ground.

Adam parked the car, and Brenna snapped her cell phone closed. Now that she'd taken care of Patch, nothing else in her evening was time-sensitive. No doubt she'd see at least a dozen people she knew inside. She'd try to reach Josh, but if he wasn't home, either, she was sure she could get a lift from someone. Maybe even someone who owned a pet and would be amenable to trading a favor in exchange for future discounts.

Geoff didn't wait for his dad to remove the keys from the ignition before bounding out of the vehicle. His sister, the moody one, took her time.

"This is the home of phenomenal food?" she asked skeptically. "Doesn't look like much."

Brenna slanted a reproving glance over her shoulder. "Friendly word of warning—don't diss the Diner within earshot of any Mistletoe natives. They'll run you out of town."

The girl pursed her lips as if she wasn't entirely certain Brenna was kidding—which she only half was. Folks around these parts took the Diner pretty seriously. The mayor's son proposed to his fiancée here over a shared dessert of gooey, sweet pecan pie.

"I'm not that hungry," Eliza finally said.

Brenna rolled her eyes inwardly; she was tempted to call the sky blue just to see what color the contrary girl would argue it was. "You may not be hungry yet, but you will be." No one, not even a rebellious preteen in the throes of a snit, could resist the smells inside.

As they strolled up the sidewalk, Brenna enumerated the local favorites on the dinner menu. After the past forty minutes of detailing great food and Mistletoe summer activities, she felt as if Belle Fulton from the Chamber of Commerce might pop up any moment to offer her a job. And Brenna was uniquely qualified to tell the Varners about the Chattavista Lodge on the outskirts of town, where they'd be staying, because her stepbrother worked there.

Josh had always been a big fan of the outdoors. In the year between her mom's defection and Maggie's illness, Brenna had lied shamelessly to Josh and Fred about her supposed love for fishing and camping, desperate to fit into the testosterone-driven household. She'd wanted to be the Perfect Daughter. *Eliza's polar opposite.* If Fred had told Brenna the sky was taupe with chartreuse polka dots, she would have agreed just to ingratiate herself with the Pierces.

These days, Brenna could appreciate the fresh air her occupation provided, but she hadn't voluntarily slept on the ground in decades. Josh had been seeing the same girl for two months, and Brenna teased him that if he wanted to keep her, he'd make sure any romantic getaways included indoor plumbing. Not that Brenna had teased him *recently*—she was currently dodging him. Now that Josh was happily in love, a newfound convert to committed relationships, he seemed gung-ho on setting up Brenna with every eligible bachelor between here and Atlanta. His girlfriend, Natalie Young, was just as bad. Of course, she was also the local florist, so she considered flourishing romances good for business.

The Diner hostess warned that there would be a short wait while someone cleaned off a table. Brenna tried reaching her stepbrother but got his voice mail, then started to call Arianne Waide but realized that, with her sister-in-law, Rachel, having a baby, Ari was probably at the hospital with the rest of the family. Brenna dialed Quinn again and left a message for her to call whenever she could. If nothing else, some local firemen she knew had just walked in and Brenna could bum a ride from them.

Considering the crowd, they were seated pretty quickly. Dinner rush at the Diner started a few minutes before five and lasted well into the night. The hostess showed them to a booth, and Morgan slid in first, followed by her father. Geoff sat opposite them and Brenna chose to sit next to the boy rather than his thoroughly attractive dad. Eliza surprised her by practically leaping in after her, sandwiching Brenna. She didn't get a strong sense that Eliza liked her, but the girl must really dislike the idea of sitting with Adam.

Had he actually done something to bring on her wrath, or was Eliza just one of those clichéd mutinous adolescents?

Fifteen minutes later, after the waitress delivered a round of lemonades and took their orders, Brenna thought she was getting a clearer picture of why the girl was so hostile. When Adam tried to draw Eliza into a discussion by asking if she would play soccer again this coming fall, the girl snorted. Brenna wondered if anyone had ever pointed out how unattractive that particular habit was.

"I haven't played soccer in two years," Eliza said, her tone reading *duh* but her expression telegraphing genuine hurt. "I play volleyball now. Mom said only two activities so that my grades don't slip, and I picked volleyball and dance."

Adam visibly cringed. "Right. I'm sorry I forgot that."

Seated on the girl's left, Brenna barely caught her muttered, "Like you even knew in the first place." Adam engaged his son in less-charged conversation about what kind of car he wanted to save up for, but then made an apparent misstep when Geoff mentioned that he couldn't wait to take his girlfriend out on an honest-to-goodness car date.

Managing not to look too nervous about that prospect, Adam asked, "So how did you and Deana meet?"

Geoff shook his head, sighing loudly, and Brenna assumed that the boy was embarrassed to have his love life be the topic of dinner conversation. But Morgan tugged on the side of Adam's shirt.

"Daddy, it's *Gina,*" she said, her little face pinched with worry. As if she feared his mistake might create even more tension. "Remember?"

Though the situations probably had nothing in common, something in the girl's voice made Brenna flash to her own past, the careful way she'd had to treat her

mother. How she'd hesitantly vacillated between reminding her mom that no, they were no longer in Lex-
ington, they'd moved on to Tennessee, and not wanting
to say anything that might set her off. As an adult looking back, Brenna suspected her mother had suffered
from some sort of bipolar disorder and hoped that,
wherever the woman was now, she'd sought help. But
as a child, Brenna had never known what to think
about her mother's moods and their nomadic lifestyle.
Brenna had spent more than a decade walking on egg-
shells—the unpleasant habit had stayed with her far
longer than her mother had.

Morgan, on the other hand, showed few signs of emotional scarring and had already bounced back from her
moment of concern. She was chanting, "Geoff and Gina.
Gina and Geoff. They both start with *G*s that think
they're *J*s. I can spell my name! Who wants to hear?"

By the time their food arrived, Morgan had spelled
out her siblings' names, as well as her own and the
words *cat, fox* and *Dan*.

"Wonderful job," Brenna praised her.

"I start kindergarten next year," Morgan said. "And
Liza's teaching me to read."

Eliza ducked her head closer to her plate of cheddar
garlic mashed potatoes as if embarrassed to be caught
doing something nice for her kid sister.

"Kindergarten?" Brenna echoed. "That must make
you, what, eleven years old?"

Morgan giggled. "Four! But I'm almost five."

Adam ruffled her hair fondly, looking more relaxed than he had since he'd first pulled over for Brenna. She imagined that sitting in front of a plate of pot roast beat the heck out of interminable hours cooped up in a car with antsy kids. "That's right," he said. "We'll have to search Mistletoe for the perfect way to celebrate your birthday next Thursday."

Eliza's fork hit the edge of her plate with a clatter. "Friday! Her birthday is Friday. Don't you even know that?"

Adam flushed darkly. "I know exactly when each one of you was born. Morgan's birthday is June twenty-sixth."

"That's Friday," Eliza said, less forcefully.

"Oh." Her father leaned back against the vinyl bench. "I was just confused about my days."

His oldest daughter nodded, while his younger daughter looked on apprehensively. Geoff continued to shovel in food at warp speed, sparing absolutely no attention for the people around him.

"I promise," Adam added. "I know every one of your birthdays. June twenty-sixth. February tenth. November third. You're the most important people in my life."

Brenna was moved by the declaration but also vaguely uncomfortable at being present for it. She was barely at ease with open sentiment in her *own* family, much less a stranger's. She focused on her fried-chicken salad with all the intensity of a grad student taking a final, but out of the corner of her eye, she saw

Adam reach across the table for Eliza's hand. And saw the girl reflexively jerk away.

Ouch.

Eliza shoved her plate to the side. She waited a beat before asking, "Can I go play air hockey? Geoff can go with me."

The boy had emptied his plate, stopping just short of licking it clean.

Reluctantly Adam nodded. "I guess. You need quarters?"

"No. Mom gave me money."

There was some shuffling as Brenna stood so that the two adolescents could get out of the booth.

"Can I go, too?" Morgan implored. "I wanna watch."

"Don't you want to finish your cheeseburger?" Adam asked.

"Nuh-uh. My tummy feels funny."

"All right. But I'll save it for later in case you change your mind." His expression was nakedly poignant as he watched his children walk away. Whatever his shortcomings, he adored those three. Brenna hoped for his sake that he found a way to convince them of that in the next few weeks.

With a sigh, Adam looked at Brenna. "You must think I'm the worst parent in the world."

"Far from it. Trust me."

"I do surgeries where another person's life is literally in my hands, and it doesn't make me half as nervous as a two-minute conversation with my daughter."

"I don't know." She feigned confusion. "Morgan didn't seem that scary to me."

His laugh was deep and appealing, and his dark eyes crinkled attractively at the corners. "Believe it or not, I—"

"Brenna!"

She turned her head, knowing her transportation dilemma had just been solved. "Josh. Hey."

Her stepbrother dropped his arm from Natalie's shoulders long enough to extend a hand across the table toward Adam. "I'm Brenna's brother, Josh Pierce."

"Dr. Adam Varner."

The two men shook, then Josh took a step back to continue the introductions, gesturing toward the very pretty blonde at his side.

"This is Natalie Young, my girlfriend," Josh said. He looked from Brenna to Adam, then back again, grinning from ear to ear. "And we are *so* glad to meet you."

Chapter Four

Brenna almost groaned at the naked joy in her stepbrother's expression. *No,* she wanted to tell him. Josh had made no secret of the fact that he wanted Brenna to date more, but Adam Varner was not an option. This was a critical time for her small company, her first potential "growth spurt," a chance to turn a profit, instead of living bill to bill each month. Brenna needed to work hard this summer, not get distracted by a man—no matter how good looking he was, or how endearing his efforts with his kids. Besides, Adam had his own summer plans and would be gone in a few weeks.

"Dr. Varner here is just passing through Mistletoe," she said quickly. "He gave me a lift when my car died. Would you and Natalie mind taking me home?"

"Of course not," Josh said absently. His bright smile had dimmed to a frown. At first Brenna thought he was upset about the car situation—he and Fred had both nagged her to let Fred cosign on a car loan. *It's no more than he would do for me,* Josh had said.

Brenna had barely stopped herself from insisting that the situation was different. Instead, she'd simply told him, "I want to be self-sufficient. *Need* to be." When you grew up subject to the whims of an unstable parent, you found that as an adult, you liked to be in control. Reliant on no one.

"So, Dr. Varner, you're an out-of-towner?" Josh asked. His tone had subtly shifted from *Welcome to the family* to *You'd better not have any outstanding warrants for your arrest.* "How convenient that you just happened to be driving by in time to pick up a lone woman in distress."

Adam looked unsure how to answer. "We were glad to be able to help."

"We?" Josh echoed, his gaze darting to Brenna. "Just how many strangers were in the car?"

She sighed. "Four, three of them not even old enough to drive. Stop looking at Dr. Varner as if he's suspect. And stop being so overprotective! *I'm* the older sibling, remember?"

"As bossy as you are," he said lightly, "how could I forget?"

Natalie politely smothered her laugh.

Adam scooted over on the bench. "Would you two like to sit down? We probably won't see my kids again until they run out of quarters."

"Thank you." Natalie sat next to him, and Josh took a seat on Brenna's side.

The waitress reappeared, clearing plates and promising a box for Morgan's cheeseburger. When she asked if Josh and Natalie needed time to decide on their orders, Josh laughed. He had the menu memorized and had probably known what he wanted even before he parked his truck out front. He asked for the barbecue plate, and after a moment's consideration, Natalie ordered a half-size fried-chicken salad.

"So, Dr. Varner…" Natalie began.

"Please, call me Adam. 'Doctor' seems too formal for vacation. And I desperately need a vacation," he added with a rueful grin.

Considering his traveling companions, Brenna doubted he'd get any real rest or relaxation.

The blonde returned his smile, her interrogation techniques a lot more amiable than Josh's. "What brings you to Mistletoe?"

"Three weeks of bonding with my kids. I have two girls and a teenage son. We're looking forward to hiking, exploring the town. We'll be staying at the Chattavista."

"What a coincidence!" Natalie said. "Josh works for the lodge."

It wasn't that big a coincidence—there were only two real places for tourists to stay around here. The Mistletoe Inn located downtown, as it were, and the more rustic Chattavista Lodge outside the town proper. Nestled among hills dotted with Georgia wildflowers, the lodge was in perfect proximity to a river that offered fishing, tubing and rafting. People made the most of outdoor sports in the spring, summer and brilliantly colored fall. During the colder months of the year, when holiday visitors were more likely to stay at the inn, the lodge offered discount space for corporate retreats, attracting businesspeople from Atlanta and surrounding states.

"I take groups out on the river," Josh said. "Well, and answer the phone and other stuff. But white-water rafting is a much more exciting job description."

Brenna smiled in his direction, feeling a big-sister rush of pride. And also feeling suddenly, inexplicably old. The quiet, shaggy-haired boy who'd seemed unsure how to react when his father married Brenna's mother was now a broad-shouldered, confident man. Despite his joking about "playing outdoors" for a living, she knew how committed he was to doing a good job. "Josh is a trained guide, a CPR instructor and a certified Wilderness First Responder."

Josh flashed a grin across the table at Natalie. "Brenna's just trying to make me sound good for you. Is it working?"

His girlfriend chuckled, but before she could reply, the waitress returned with their food.

Josh offered his heartfelt thanks, then stole a glance at Brenna. There was a mischievous gleam in his eye. "Now, if I wanted to repay the favor and make Brenna sound good for anyone's benefit, I might mention how she kept making the dean's list and got her MBA."

Apparently he'd weighed the potential risks of Adam's being a total stranger against the likelihood of

Brenna finding another boyfriend soon and had come down in favor of the good doctor.

Well, can't fault his taste, anyway.

"You have an MBA?" Adam asked, looking at Brenna in surprise.

Some people found it perplexing that she'd busted her butt for six years in higher education and now walked dogs. "I interned at a corporation after I got my bachelor's, then tried jobs at two other places once I completed my MBA. After three false starts, I realized that cubicles and Monday-morning meetings just aren't for me. I lack the corporate group-think mentality." More alarmingly, she'd felt restless, edgy. For the first time in her life, she'd worried about turning into her mother, so she'd abruptly quit and come "home" to Mistletoe, wanting to feel grounded.

And it had worked. Creating her own business from the ground up was challenging but immensely satisfying; she was carving out her own unique place among family and friends. "My MBA isn't being wasted, though. I am my own marketing staff, HR and accounting department."

"Lot of responsibility," Adam said.

"It's not exactly on a par with heart surgery," she said with a wry smile, "but I am very aware that people are trusting me with keys to their homes and members of their family." Furry, four-legged members, but still.

"Dad!" Geoff yelled from the middle of the dining room. Adam whipped his head around as if anticipating an emergency, but Geoff's chief concern as he ambled toward them seemed to be, "Any food left?"

Adam stopped his son as he reached for the white square box on the table. "That is your sister's. And I know your mother raised you with better manners. You don't shout across a restaurant unless it's urgent."

Looking genuinely bemused, Geoff asked, "Was I shouting? Sorry."

"Now say hello to Brenna's brother, Josh, and his friend Natalie."

"Hey." Geoff nodded politely to Josh, then turned to Natalie. Whereupon he reddened and looked away.

Brenna managed not to smile. When Natalie had been in high school, she'd been one of the head cheerleaders, admired by many tongue-tied teenage boys; a decade later, she was still a head-turner. "We were just telling your father that Josh is a river guide. You have any interest in white-water rafting?"

"That would be *awe*some!" Geoff sat next to Josh, temporarily forgetting Natalie's good looks and even food. "Dad, can we try that while we're here? I know you said we'll go fishing and tubing, but can we try rafting, too?"

Dumb, Bren. Seeing Geoff's animated expression, she realized that she shouldn't have said something before finding out if it was okay with Adam. It was akin to asking someone else's dog, "Wanna go for a walk?" and getting it all excited without knowing whether the owner had time for that.

"I don't know." Adam sounded dubious but refrained from shooting her any accusatory glances. "How old do you have to be to do that, Josh?"

"For rafting, the minimum age is seven. It goes up from there, depending on the intensity of the trip you sign up for."

Adam nodded. "Morgan's way too young."

Speaking of which. Brenna noticed the girls threading their way through the dining room.

"I was still playing," Morgan announced forlornly, "but Eliza said I couldn't stay back there by myself."

"She's absolutely right," Adam said.

"She said she wanted to come find out who the he—"

"So is there still room at the table for us?" Eliza asked, blushing furiously.

Adam gave her a hard look, then sighed. "Grab a couple of chairs from that empty table over there. You can sit on the end, and Morgan can squeeze in here with me."

It was a perfectly reasonable suggestion since Morgan took up no room, and Eliza, having already eaten, didn't need much space. But she looked so ticked off that Adam might as well have asked her to sleep on the floor so someone else could have her bed. From what Brenna had seen so far, it would be easy to believe Eliza was just ticked off at the world in general. But Brenna thought there was more to it than that.

Although the girl acted as if she loathed her father, was she jealous of his attention elsewhere? Eliza already had to share him with two siblings, and now, on the very first day of their vacation, three new people were added to the mix.

Brenna thought of the string of boyfriends with whom she'd had to compete for her mother's scattered attention—until the woman had left her outright. "Josh, I don't suppose you're ready to leave?"

As she finished the question, he gaped at her. He wasn't even halfway finished with his meal. "You in a hurry?"

"I…" Between her attraction to Adam and her discomfort at being the outsider witnessing another family's drama, she couldn't be more eager to go. But since she couldn't say any of that, she concluded, "I still have one stop tonight in my neighborhood, and I should try and go by the Dillingers' if I can get a ride over there. Plus, I have a lot of clerical stuff to catch up on tonight. I've been so busy with the actual pet visits for the last few days that I'm behind on updating my calendar, printing invoices and logging checks to deposit." Which was crucial since it looked as though she'd have to rent a car while hers was being fixed. Lord alone knew how much *that* was going to set her back.

"We can take the rest of our dinner to go," Natalie offered.

"No, that's all right." Brenna backpedaled, feeling silly and ungrateful. "You guys are doing me the favor. The least I can do is let you finish your meal."

"Nobody rush on our account," Adam said. "The kids and I should actually head out to the lodge. If I wait until it gets dark, I may end up lost. Natalie, Josh, it was nice meeting both of you."

"I'll definitely see you around," Josh said. "If you want, I can recommend activities for your whole family."

"Thanks." Adam's gaze fell on Brenna. "And maybe I'll see you around this summer, too?"

"Don't count on it," Josh said, shooting her a teasing smile. "Her workdays sometimes start as early as five and can go past ten o'clock. She has no life."

Brenna sucked in a breath, a bit embarrassed that Adam had heard her described that way. She briefly considered smacking her stepbrother upside the head, but violence was a bad example for the children.

Besides, it probably wasn't fair to get mad at someone just for speaking the truth.

"QUINN, DO YOU THINK I have no life?"

The brunette driving the car stifled a yawn. "It's not even seven in the morning and my coffee hasn't kicked in yet. I'm not thinking *anything*."

Brenna stared at the day's schedule and said nothing. As it was, she couldn't believe she was letting Josh's comment from the night before bother her. She'd known going into the summer that she would have next to no free time, and it hadn't disturbed her then. So why was it eating at her now?

Because you felt pathetic in front of Adam Varner?

That was a ludicrous reaction. After all, aside from their paths potentially crossing at the Diner or Mistletoe's only sizable grocery store, she wasn't planning to see him again. How he viewed her lifestyle was immaterial.

"Brenna? Everything okay?" Quinn asked, sounding more alert.

"Yeah, just ignore me. Everything's fine—except my car." The local automobile dealership also rented vehicles, but when she'd called yesterday evening, they'd said she would have to wait until noon to pick one up. That would be useful for her afternoon visits, not so much for the various dogs who'd been home alone since last night and *really* needed to be let out this morning. "I appreciate your helping me out today."

"No problem," Quinn said. "Honestly, it's good for me. With school out for the summer, I've turned into a bum and sleep in way too late most days. Besides…"

"Yes?" Brenna prompted.

Quinn laughed. "I feel like an idiot saying this out loud, but I'm happy for the excuse not to be at home this morning. I hired Gabriel Sloan to do some roof repair for me. I'm lucky that last set of storms didn't leave me with a living room full of water. Dylan's pretty handy and does as much work around my half of the duplex as his own, but he and Chloe are away at Hilton Head." Dylan Echols was coach of the Mistletoe High baseball team; until tryouts in late July, he, like Quinn, had the summer free.

"Gabe Sloan, huh?" Since the man didn't own a pet, Brenna didn't know him very well. But most everyone in Mistletoe knew *of* him.

"Yeah. He does great work and you can't find a fairer price, but I get a little unnerved around him. Not because of the scandal—that's ancient history and probably got exaggerated in gossip, anyway. It's just that he's so *intense*. Lilah says she's never noticed." Lilah Waide was Quinn's best friend.

Brenna laughed. "That's because Lilah's too wrapped up in that hunky husband of hers to notice anything about other men."

"Arianne said that, too. Except she didn't refer to her brother as 'hunky.' But she does think Gabriel is sexy."

"Really?"

Arianne, Lilah's sister-in-law, had grown up with two older brothers; she was chatty, opinionated and socially fearless. The idea of Ari having a conversation with the brooding loner Gabe Sloan was both vastly entertaining and completely unimaginable.

"Oh!" Brenna snapped her fingers. "I forgot to ask. How are Rachel and the baby doing?"

Quinn smiled. "Wonderfully. Arianne called me from the hospital last night to say that Bailey Kathryn Waide is beautiful and that the entire family is already wrapped around her teeny tiny finger. David should be taking home both his ladies this afternoon."

"You should have seen him yesterday when he stopped to see if I needed a ride." Brenna smiled at the memory. She'd gone to school with the eldest Waide sibling; he'd been the valedictorian of her graduating class. "I always thought he was unflappable, but he looked terrified."

Quinn rolled to a stop at a red light. "I want to hear more about the guy who *did* give you a ride. Single dad, huh? Was he good-looking?"

Oh, yeah. "I suppose. He's only in town for a few weeks, though."

"A lot could happen in that time," Quinn said playfully. "I don't want to sound desperate, but I've lived here my whole life. I've already met most of the local prospects. You ever worry about that?"

"Umm…" Brenna spent more time worrying about whether she'd met most of the pet-owners in Mistletoe.

"There are a lot of great guys here in Mistletoe," Quinn continued. "Even a few that are still single. But if I were going to click with someone, feel that *spark,* shouldn't it have happened by now?"

Brenna tried to think back to her last real relationship, her only serious one since returning to Mistletoe. But it had never gotten as serious as Kevin would have liked. Had there been a definitive spark between her and Kevin Higgs?

The vet was handsome, definitely, and had been a considerate lover. They'd had common interests and enjoyed each other's company, but in retrospect, she wasn't sure her feelings for him had been strong enough to generate real chemistry.

"The thing about sparks, Quinn, is that they can lead to fire."

"Exactly! Igniting passion, that all-consuming heat when you're around just the right guy."

Maybe Quinn would be comfortable with that kind of volatility, but Brenna would be frantically looking around for an extinguisher. "Well, good luck with the chemistry thing. For me, right now all I want is to grow my business and expand my client base." She'd hoped to start building a nest egg, eventually hire part-time help, but her transportation needs were an even more pressing priority.

"Hmm." Quinn shot her a sidelong glance. "So…if you're all satisfied and fulfilled with just your work, why the question about whether or not you have a life?"

"This is why I like dogs and cats," Brenna grumbled. "They don't point out any conversational inconsistencies!"

Quinn laughed. "In other words, I should shut up and drive?"

"Please."

"DA-AD!" GEOFF'S VOICE echoed through the two-bedroom suite, an indignant demand for justice.

Adam rubbed the space between his eyes. "What seems to be the problem, Geoff?" The *current* problem.

It was now eight-thirty. At two o'clock this morning, the problem had been that Morgan missed her mom and was scared in the unfamiliar bedroom the girls shared, even though Adam had left a closet light on for her. She'd crawled into Eliza's bed, which led to Eliza complaining at three-fifteen that Morgan kicked in her sleep. So he'd given up his own bed for his disgruntled daughter and stretched out on the small sofa in the common room. At seven, he'd awoken to a stiff neck and a bright-eyed Morgan wanting to know why she couldn't find her regular cartoons. The small television in the common room had basic cable but not the array of personalized channels Morgan was used to at home.

"It'll be all right," he'd assured her. "We won't spend that much time in the suite, anyway."

He'd promised them a hearty breakfast in the lodge's main dining hall if everyone could manage to get ready.

Geoff flung out his arm, pointing at the bathroom door. "The problem is we've got only one bathroom, and Eliza seems to think it's her sole dominion."

"What's do-min-on?" Morgan asked. She'd insisted on picking out her own clothes, pairing a red shirt covered in pink animal shapes with neon-striped leggings. The overall effect, best described as *colorful,* was not helping Adam's headache. "Is it like a dalmatian?"

"No, pumpkin." Adam knocked on the bathroom door. "Eliza?"

The door swung open. "Jeez, I'm finished," she said from around her father, glaring at Geoff. "Happy now?"

Mumbling a response, Geoff dashed into the now vacant room. He shut the door with just enough force to up Adam's need for aspirin without technically slamming it.

Ten minutes later, all three children were ready to go, even if one of them looked like the inside of a kaleidoscope and another was wearing too much eye makeup. Sara had discussed the cosmetics issue with him just before Eliza's twelfth birthday and he'd deferred to Sara's judgment, saying that if she was okay with it, so was he. But he wasn't an idiot. He knew that Eliza didn't leave the house with red lipstick and raccoon eyes on her mother's watch. She was baiting him, but he refused to kick off their morning with a fight.

He held the door open while the kids filed past, dropping a gentle hand on Eliza's shoulder.

"What?" Her voice, probably meant to be challenging, came out nervous and guilty.

"I love you, kiddo."

She blinked, the little girl he remembered peering out from inside a ring of uneven eyeliner. Then she was gone. "Y-yeah, I know. We better go. If Geoff doesn't get fed soon, he'll probably start eating the furniture or something."

With that, she darted into the hall. Adam sighed. *The Medical College Admission Test was easier than this.*

The good news? It was bound to get better.

Chapter Five

"And I assume you want to pay extra for the unlimited miles?" Lloyd asked from behind the counter.

Honestly, Brenna thought, *no one ever* wants *to pay extra for anything.* But she did accumulate an amazingly high mileage for a woman who spent most of her time driving around a small town, and tomorrow was Saturday. Weekends were often her busiest time. "Same deal as last time, please. Extra mileage, extra insurance."

Lloyd grinned at her. "You're one of our favorite customers. Which is really saying something considering you've never purchased a car from us. I'll be right back with the finalized paperwork and your receipt."

"Thanks."

Brenna had bought Quinn an early lunch to thank her for her assistance that morning, and Quinn had dropped her off at the auto dealership.

"Sure you don't want me to keep chauffeuring you?" her friend had asked.

"Thanks, but my schedule's a bit erratic for the next forty-eight hours." The Hildebrand family was paying her an exorbitant fee to "tuck in" their chocolate Lab for the night; she'd check on him one last time at about ten-thirty. "I can't just keep you at my beck and call."

"All right, guess I'll head home. But don't tell Ari we parted ways this early. She was angling shamelessly for an invitation to come hang out at my place and catch glimpses of Gabe in his work jeans." Quinn had waved goodbye with a reminder to "call if you need me."

"Brenna!"

At the sound of her stepfather's voice, she spun around. The sight of his rugged face filled her with affection and exasperation. *Josh, you twerp.* She'd bet the cost of her latest phone-book ad that Josh had told his parents about her unreliable car.

"Hey." She hugged Fred. "Didn't expect to see you here." Although she should have.

He patted her on the back. "I don't suppose you'd believe I just happened to be in the neighborhood?"

She sighed. "Well, it *is* Mistletoe. I guess the neighborhood's not *that* big."

"I've offered to go car shopping with you a couple of times, honey, and you're always too busy. So what better time than now? You're here, I'm here. An entire lot of economy cars await."

"You know I appreciate the thought." Mostly. "But I need to get over to the Heritage Pond subdivision. I've got a new-client orientation at twelve-thirty."

"Got time in your full schedule for Sunday dinner? Josh and Natalie are coming. Maggie's hoping you can join us, too."

She ground her back teeth. On the one hand, she loved the Pierces and enjoyed spending time with them, but Fred and Maggie had already been trying to help her find "a nice man" even before Josh started dating Natalie. Now all four of them ganged up on her. And she was the fifth wheel, the odd one out even among people who adored her.

She was damn lucky for the Pierce family and never wanted to seem ungrateful. "You tell Maggie I'll be there. Can I bring anything?"

"Just your company and your lovely smile," Fred said warmly. "Unless…there's any*one* you wanted to bring? Any guest of yours is always welcome at our table."

"Oh, for pity's sake! Josh couldn't just leave it at tattling about the car? He told you about the doctor, too!"

"Doctor?" Fred frowned. "What doctor?"

Whoops. She'd read too much into Fred and Maggie's habitual wishful thinking, immediately making the mental leap to handsome Adam Varner.

"Never mind," Brenna chirped brightly. "Not important."

"But—"

"Okay, you're all set," Lloyd said from behind them.

"Wonderful! Thanks!" Beaming at him, she accepted the keys to the getaway car.

Since she'd already cited a customer appointment,

her stepfather had no choice but to let her go. Unexpectedly her thoughts of Adam were harder to shake. She'd been moved yesterday by his desire to bond with his kids—undoubtedly he'd been an imperfect father, but the fact that he was trying so hard counted for a lot with her. *Wonder if he's having any luck yet.*

ADAM LEANED on the railing of the lodge's massive wraparound wooden porch, listening to intermittent birdsong and the burbling rush of the river. Behind him, Geoff and Eliza were trying to teach Morgan how to play checkers. In a minute he'd join them, but he hated to push his luck. The day so far had exceeded his most optimistic expectations.

A few months ago, he'd kept the kids for an afternoon while Sara and Dan were busy with wedding plans. When Sara had come to pick up the children, she'd caught Adam in a moment of extreme frustration with Eliza; he'd confessed to his ex-wife that he'd never felt so clueless in his life. She'd told him, with a mix of compassion and censure, that half of parenting was just showing up. Today had certainly borne that out. *Thank God.*

When he'd proposed coming to Mistletoe, even Sara had been surprised by his choice of location. There were plenty of great places in Tennessee— Gatlinburg, Pigeon Forge or Chattanooga were far more obvious tourist destinations—but he hadn't wanted to take the kids anywhere they'd already been. He'd wanted the four of them to have a vacation uniquely their own.

Day one, while not yet over, seemed a success. After a buffet breakfast, they'd followed a trail into the woods. It hadn't been too steep or overgrown for Morgan to keep up, but it wasn't so perfectly manicured that they might as well have been walking on a sidewalk in their own subdivision. Even surly Eliza had been charmed by the sight of a mother deer and fawn in a clearing. They'd also spotted lizards, chipmunks and the white cottontail of a rabbit that'd taken off at the sound of Morgan's delighted squeal.

Their lunch back at the lodge had been a lively exchange of everyone's favorite moments. Now the kids wore bathing suits under their clothes, and he'd promised to take them swimming after their food had settled. They probably wouldn't hit the river until tomorrow or the next day, but the lodge also had a good-size pool with a high, winding waterslide. He'd noticed that when Eliza ducked into the bathroom to put on her suit, she'd also wiped off that awful makeup, which he opted to see as a sign of truce.

"You can't jump my piece from there," Geoff said to Morgan, shaking his head over the checkerboard. "Remember how I already explained that to you?"

Geoff sounded as if he had a reserve of patience. Adam decided to intervene while that was still the case. "Who's ready for the pool?"

"Me!" the kids chorused.

Geoff took the checkers back to the front desk while Eliza helped her little sister apply sunscreen. Once they were inside the fenced pool area, they took turns passing back and forth the tube of SPF 55. Adam prided himself on not doing an aghast double take when Eliza removed her long T-shirt and revealed an electric-blue bikini. It wasn't so much the cut of the suit that was disconcerting—as two pieces went, he supposed it was modest enough—it was how much older she suddenly looked. His little girl, far too grown up. He wondered if there was any chance Morgan would humor him and wear a one-piece into her twenties.

They had the pool practically to themselves. A man slept beneath the shade of an umbrella, a brunette read a book on her chaise longue, and a mother sat on the steps of the shallow end while her toddler repeatedly filled with water and dumped out a purple plastic pail. The lifeguard, a boy of about sixteen, looked bored to pieces.

Or at least he did until Eliza balled up her shirt and stuck it in the duffel bag.

She's twelve! Adam wanted to scream. Rather than do so, Adam settled for a dark glower in the punk's direction.

Geoff and Eliza both went immediately for the waterslide, but Morgan was more tentative. She got in the water slowly, step by step, seeking frequent reassurance that her dad would stay close. Once she'd made it all the way into the pool, she wanted him to help her practice floating on her back. She made swift progress with that and had moved on to a clumsy but solo back-stroke when she announced in a panicked whisper that she needed to go potty.

The nearest restrooms were in a bathhouse midway between the pool and a river dock. "Geoff, Eliza! I'll be right back," Adam called.

Morgan slid on her shoes, then tucked her hand in his. "I'm having fun," she told him. "You should come on trips with us and Mommy and Daddy Dan."

"Or maybe you can just alternate. Take turns," he clarified. "Go somewhere with them, then some-where else with me. That way you get twice as many vacations."

"Okay. Hey, know what I want for my birthday?" She kept up a running commentary for the duration of their stroll, and Adam realized he didn't even miss the hospital. He hadn't thought about any of his patients today or wondered how his eminently qualified col-leagues were doing filling in for him. Waiting by a restroom door while his preschooler cheerfully called out the name of every My Special Puppy in the Pup-pydale toy collection, he wouldn't want to be anywhere else in the world.

It was a nonsensical, trivial moment—except that it was a moment in Morgan's life.

On their return trip to the pool, Morgan suddenly shrieked, "Kitty!" and darted off the path. "Daddy, did you see it?"

He caught her elbow before she stumbled over a

rock. "Can't say that I did. Remember what we talked about, that animals are scared by loud noises?"

Her face puckered into a worried scowl. "It shouldn't be here with the river down the hill and the pool. Cats can't swim."

"They can," he told her. "Most of them just prefer not to. I'm sure the cat will be fine."

She hesitated, unconvinced, but ultimately resumed her pace. It took Adam two tries to unlatch the gate because his attention was zeroed in on his other daughter. That punk lifeguard had climbed down from his elevated chair and stood entirely too close to Eliza.

Bionic-father hearing kicked in and Adam eavesdropped, only missing a few words here and there, while the kid boasted of how he'd had his driver's license for months and planned to buy a "second generation" Camaro from a family friend at the end of the summer. Eliza—who usually rolled her eyes whenever Geoff waxed rhapsodic about automobiles—morphed into a Devoted Car Enthusiast, all oohs and ahhs and big brown eyes.

Geoff took Morgan to play on the waterslide, so Adam sat down and tried to relax. He noticed the brunette sunbather in the halter-top suit smiling in his direction; reflexively, he smiled back and she gave a coquettish little finger wave. She was attractive, he noted objectively, but she was no Brenna Pierce.

He frowned, recalling Eliza's indignation that he might try to steal time from their family vacation to make room for romance. *Definitely not.* He'd unintentionally made his children feel as if they weren't a top priority, and this trip was a major step in reversing that. Ironic, though, that Eliza had lectured him less than twenty-four hours ago when she clearly had no qualms about abandoning her family to chat up a bronzed man-child whose smirk bordered on predatory.

Reminding himself that Eliza was in plain sight and therefore perfectly safe, Adam dug a medical journal out of his bag. He even made a halfhearted attempt to read an article about the rise of robot-assisted cardiothoracic procedures. Mostly he skimmed while keeping one ear on his daughter and the punk. *Minimized trauma, reduced risk of infection.*

"So, have you ever, like, *saved* anyone?" Eliza asked.

"Sure. Just last week I jumped in to rescue a lady with a cramp in her leg. And this kid who panicked and was flailing like crazy."

Faster recovery time, wave of the future, blah, blah, blah.

"But I've never given mouth-to-mouth," Punk added smarmily. "At least, not in the line of duty. During my off-hours—"

Adam shot out of his chair, tipping it sideways with his sudden movement. It clattered against the pavement, drawing the notice of just about everyone—including his daughter and the punk lifeguard at whom he happened to be glaring. *Now what, O Father of the Year?*

He hadn't really leaped up with any sort of plan. It

had simply been an instinctive reaction. But judging from the mingled horror and fury settling across his daughter's face, that explanation was not going to mollify her. Especially since it would involve him admitting that he'd been listening to her private conversation in the first place.

"Uh…" The lifeguard glanced from Adam back to Eliza, his earlier smirk gone. Looking pale beneath his tan, the kid jerked his thumb up at the elevated seat. "I'd better get back to work."

"Yeah. Nice talking to you," Eliza said through gritted teeth. She ducked her head, her shoulders slumping slightly as if she was curling in on herself in hopes of becoming invisible, and stalked toward her father.

Adam assumed she was making a beeline for confrontation, but her gait never slowed as she neared. Instead, she strode past, exiting the pool area. He experienced a stab of indecision so intense it was almost panic. Should he give her space? For all he knew, she was excusing herself to go to the bathhouse for an adolescent cry. *That* you *caused.* Then again, did he know for an absolute certainty that she wouldn't do something dramatic like run away? Try to hitch back to Tennessee?

This was excruciating. In the O.R., he didn't second-guess himself. He took decisive actions and saved lives.

"Geoff, keep your sister in the shallow end until I get back," he called over his shoulder. Giving a girl "space" might sound like a sensitive, insightful parenting move, but Adam rejected it after a moment's thought. She was *twelve*. While she might have the right to be angry with him, she did not have the same right to storm off alone into the forest or down toward the river.

"Eliza!" Though she didn't overtly speed up to evade him, she didn't stop, either. "Hey, I know you hear me. Slow down so we can talk about this."

When she actually did stop, he released a tense breath. He hadn't known if she would—or what he'd do in the face of direct disobedience.

She whipped her head around, and his heart clutched at the sight of her watery eyes. "I don't *want* to talk to you. I don't even want to be here! I could have stayed with friends while Mom and Dan are away."

Adam tried not to take her words personally. Didn't all children go through an "I hate you" phase as an automatic part of growing up and wrestling with independence? "This trip wasn't about your mom needing a babysitter. It was about me wanting to spend time with you guys."

"Do you even care what *we* want? Geoff was freaked out when you said you were taking us away for so long. He's worried Gina will meet someone else before we get back. And Morgan—"

"—is having a blast. She told me so herself. I think if you give this vacation a chance, we could all have fun."

"I was trying to! I was making a new friend. A cute friend who probably wants nothing to do with me now that you practically lunged at him from across the pool."

"I… He was too old for you."

She snorted. "Oh, I didn't know there were age limits for who I was allowed to talk to!"

"I'm sorry I upset you, but I'm still your father. Rein in the sarcasm."

When she opened her mouth to retort, he braced himself, but no scathing reply came. Her tears brimmed over, escalating quickly to actual sobs. She covered her face with her hands.

"What can I do?" Adam asked softly. "We're together for the next eighteen days, and I don't want it to be miserable for you. What can I do to make it better?"

She sniffed. "Just give me the room key. Please? I want to go lie down."

"All right." He handed over the key ring bearing the Chattavista logo—no modern key cards here. "Lock the door behind you, though. I'll get a spare from the front desk later."

"Fine."

When he turned back toward the pool, he was surprised to find Geoff and Morgan watching through the fence, both their faces apprehensive.

"You guys tired of swimming?" he asked, heading toward them.

Morgan held up her hands. "I'm getting wrinkly. The lady who gave us the checkers game said she had coloring books, too."

Fifteen minutes later, she was happily coloring pictures of farm animals back on the lodge porch. Adam and Geoff sat at a nearby table, setting up a game of backgammon.

"Geoff…when I told you guys about this trip, did you want to come?"

The teenager flinched. "Th-this trip?"

Adam got a sinking feeling in the pit of his stomach. "It's okay, son. You can tell me the truth."

Geoff looked away. "I like fishing. And it would be really cool to go rafting."

"Do you miss Gina?"

"Well, yeah, I guess." He seemed surprised by the question. "But, jeez, it's only been two days. It's just…most of the other guys are like that bozo back at the pool, working summer jobs to save up for a car. Not to mention cash for the movies and music downloads and stuff. Mom lets me cut lawns and stuff in the neighborhood, but she won't let me apply for any real jobs during the school year."

And Adam had thoughtlessly wiped out three weeks of prime earning potential. *Hell.* "I guess you're at an age where I can't say I'm sorry with ice cream?"

Geoff eyed the backgammon pieces. "Do you mind if I take a rain check on this? I think I'm gonna go back to the room and catch the Braves game on TV."

"Sure. Don't turn it up too loud, though. Your sister might be taking a nap."

And then there was one.

Deflated, Adam joined Morgan and helped her polka-dot animals. She'd started with a dalmatian and decided to continue the theme with a green-speckled cow and purple-spotted sheep.

"Daddy!"

"Yeah, pumpkin?"

She lowered her voice to an excited whisper. "There it is! My kitty!"

Sure enough, peeking out from the edge of some bushes was a small, charcoal-colored cat. Adam couldn't get a clear look at it among the leaves and branches, but he could tell there was no collar.

"Here, kitty." Morgan made some soft noises, a combination of tongue-clucks and kissing sounds.

The feline cocked its head, then took a few tentative steps forward with its front legs low to the ground. Its mew was plaintive.

Morgan's pale blue eyes lit up with joy. "Daddy, it answered me!" She shot to her feet, then headed down the stairs.

"Now wait just a second. You can't just go up to strange animals." Not that the tiny piece of fluff looked feral or rabid.

Even though his warning slowed Morgan—she stood immobile on the bottom step—it did nothing to deter the young cat. It crept forward, mewing again with more volume.

"That's what I want for my birthday!" Morgan announced. "A *real* pet, not just another stuffed animal. Please, Daddy?"

Any other day, Adam probably could have found the

willpower to say no, despite her beseeching expression. At this particular instant, after feeling like a failure with both Eliza and Geoff, the best he could come up with was a feeble, "It might already have an owner."

"But if it doesn't?" she pressed.

He hadn't let them keep a dog at his place because he wasn't there often enough to walk it, but weren't cats more self-sufficient? "I don't know, pumpkin. But..."

"But?"

"We'll see."

The cat, hardly more than a kitten, had reached the stairs. It propped its front feet on the step and bumped Morgan's foot with its head. She immediately knelt down to pet it, earning a trilling purr that didn't sound the least bit melancholy or unsure.

To Adam's ear, it sounded triumphant.

Chapter Six

"More than Puppy Love, Brenna Pierce speaking." Brenna sandwiched the cell phone between her ear and shoulder so that her hands were free to put the lettuce in Sheldon's terrarium.

"Brenna? This is Adam Varner."

She was stunned. With a dozen clients coming and going from town and calling with last-minute requests or schedule changes, the doctor's voice had been the last one she'd expected to hear. "Hi. How are things at the Chattavista?"

"Complicated," he said wryly. "I'm calling about the most recent complication, in fact. I…wondered if we could hire you."

For what? He'd joked yesterday about being desperate, but the only "children" she babysat were furry, feathered or scaly. "I don't understand. Unless you've suddenly acquired a pet between now and when I saw you last, I don't think I'm your—"

"We seem to be the proud owners of a cat," he

informed her. "Lydia, the lady working the desk here, said it's the third young cat to show up around here in the last couple of weeks. There was probably a litter nearby. Morgan's pushing for us to take it home as a family pet—made that her explicit birthday wish—but even if we do, the lodge allows only service animals in the rooms. I don't suppose you ever board animals for clients?"

"Sometimes," she admitted. Josh teased her that she had the sole guest room in Mistletoe specifically decorated for four-legged guests. "But only under certain conditions." Any animal she took into her home had to be smaller than her border collie, spayed or neutered, on preventative treatment for parasites, housebroken and good-natured. Even though she kept visiting pets in a room separate from where her own dog and cat lived when she wasn't there to supervise, she refused to take chances with aggressive animals.

"I'm sure you're busy," he began, "so I hate to bother you with this. We'll pay whatever you think is fair."

She grinned. "Shouldn't you ask what that is first?"

"No, I'm putting myself completely in your hands. Well, yours and a veterinarian's. Do you know a good veterinarian?"

Her face warmed. "Yes, very well. I used to work for him."

"Is there any chance he's open late on Fridays?" Adam asked on a sigh, sounding as if he already knew the answer.

Brenna bit the inside of her lip. "Actually, they close the office at four-thirty on Fridays, but he works from nine to twelve on Saturdays."

Of course, Saturdays tended to be quite busy and he'd only bump an animal with an appointment if there was an unavoidable emergency. The idea of asking her ex-boyfriend for a favor was about as pleasant as acid indigestion. Still, she did owe Adam for helping out her and Patch yesterday. She liked to keep her karmic balance sheet even. "Let me get off the phone, and I'll call Dr. Higgs. I think I can get him to squeeze you in after hours. Lydia or Josh will give you directions. It's Dr. Kevin Higgs."

"Thank you." Simple words, but there was a wealth of relief in his voice. He had obviously been worried about disappointing his children.

Considering that she didn't know him well, it was disconcertingly easy to imagine his expression, the gratitude in those dark eyes, the smile on his face.

"I'll see you there," Brenna said, wishing she wasn't so eagerly looking forward to it.

In the back seat—where all three children had opted to sit—debate raged about what to call the cat. Morgan's top choices seemed to be Hannah and Strawberry. Geoff, who had the cat in his lap, had scoffed that, as cats were distant cousins of lions and tigers, the dark gray bundle of fur needed a "tougher" name.

"Why don't we hold off on a name?" Adam suggested not for the first time. "Dr. Higgs needs to check her out, make sure she's not sick. And even if she's perfectly healthy, the vet might know who she belongs to. What if she has owners who are worried about her?"

The cat was so thin, Adam doubted she had recently enjoyed a home, but she was undeniably comfortable with people. Lydia had found them a cardboard box; they'd set the cat inside, loosely swaddled in a beach towel to hamper any escape attempts. But she only stretched up out of her snug confines when someone stopped petting her. Adam could hear the purring in the front seat.

"We haven't named her," Eliza said. "We're just discussing possibilities." She sounded hopeful rather than hostile. Any lingering anger she felt over the pool incident had dissipated when she'd seen the young cat in Adam's hands.

"That must be the place!" Geoff said, pointing. "I see Ms. Pierce."

To their left, three storefronts—a crafts shop, a ballet studio and Dr. Higgs's office—shared a parking lot. Brenna sat on the front bumper of a white sedan; the only other vehicle outside the vet's office was a blue truck. Adam parked next to Brenna.

"Nobody open any doors!" he cautioned. "Just because the cat's been calm up until now doesn't mean she won't try to make a break for it. The last thing we want is for her to be running onto the street. Geoff, wait for me to come around and help you with the box."

"Yes, sir."

Sir? The kids must really, *really* want a pet.

Adam had to admit, the idea was growing on him. It would give the kids an extra reason to visit, give him a conversation starter when he didn't know what to say to them, which happened more frequently than he cared to admit. While Morgan was the most vocal about wanting to keep the cat, her big sister clearly felt the same way. What would it be like if the next time Eliza came over she actually *smiled?*

Before opening the car door to the potential chaos of cat and kids, he took the quiet moment as an opportunity to thank Brenna. "I really appreciate your meeting us."

"Don't mention it. Always willing to go the extra mile for a new client." She said it casually, but he found himself mentally replaying the statement, trying to put his finger on something—the way he might hum a song when he was trying to remember its title.

"So did Dr. Higgs agree to see us?" he asked.

Brenna straightened away from the bumper, standing. "I was lucky enough to catch his receptionist before she left. Winnie's got the softest heart of anyone I've ever met. She not only harangued him into staying late, I think she actually got you a discount on his services. She probably deserves your thanks more than I do. I've barely done anything."

It clicked then, that vibe he'd been trying to pinpoint. Something in Brenna's manner reminded him of a cardiac resident he'd once worked with—a gifted surgeon who, while professional and superficially amiable, had maintained an intangible emotional barrier between herself and her patients. It was a necessary part of the profession. Something in the way Brenna had immediately classified him as a "client," the way she'd tried to give Winnie the credit for helping him, as if to distance herself personally.

Or maybe he was too quick to make the analogy, too used to being surrounded by doctors and nurses who were virtually required to keep others at a friendly arm's length.

"I'd better get the kids and the cat." He opened the back door, wedging himself in the space as much as possible in case the cat startled them all by bolting. Cats were quick, and this one was small enough to disappear into tight spaces. Adam didn't relish the thought of diving for her as she tore across the asphalt.

He needn't have worried. Though she stopped purring and eyed him warily, she remained immobile inside the box. He backed away so that the children could file out of the car.

"Hey, guys." Brenna smiled at the kids, then leaned closer to peer over Adam's shoulder at the cat. "Hi, there." Her voice was a low, soothing murmur. "Aren't you a sweetie?"

The cat began purring again, blinking up at Brenna with admiration, and Adam found himself grinning. He knew how the cat felt.

As they all walked toward the building, Morgan

asked questions about what the vet would do. When Brenna explained that their cat would probably receive vaccinations for rabies, distemper and feline leukemia, Morgan winced in sympathy.

"Shots hurt," she complained. Her voice quavered. "After my birthday, when we get back to Tennessee, I have to have shots, too."

"I'll bet you'll be really brave," Brenna said, holding the door open for them.

"Prob'ly not," Morgan said. "I cried last time, but my mom got me ice cream. Daddy, do you think you can take me to the doctor's this time?"

Adam paused, glancing over his shoulder. "I don't know, pumpkin." He would need to check his schedule—her five-year checkup was undoubtedly right after their return, and he was already missing an unprecedented amount of work.

Her face fell.

"Maybe I can," he said. "I *want* to. I just—"

"It's okay, Daddy."

Eliza put her arm around Morgan's shoulders and pulled her little sister closer. It made his heart hurt, the idea that his kids had to comfort one another because he let them down. Getting them a cat only made up for so much.

Inside the empty reception area, Brenna called, "Hello?"

A door opened at the other end of a hallway covered in posters of dogs and cats. "Back here, just finishing some paperwork," a male voice answered. Seconds later, a tall man wearing a lab coat over a polo shirt and jeans appeared. Well over six feet, he had short, black hair worn with sideburns and extremely light eyes. "Hello, Brenna. And these must be the Varners?"

"I'm Morgan!"

The man bent down closer to her level. "I'm Dr. Higgs. How 'bout we go back to one of the exam rooms and make sure this kitty cat of yours is healthy?"

"Okay! My daddy's a doctor, too. But he only takes care of *humans,*" she said dismissively.

Adam felt rather than heard Brenna's muffled laugh. He turned in her direction with a sternly raised eyebrow, but the truth was, he enjoyed the mischievous sparkle in her expression. Lord, she was pretty.

"The rooms are kind of small," Brenna said. "Rather than all of us trying to squeeze in, I'll just wait out here."

The vet studied her for a long moment.

"Can I stay with Ms. Pierce?" Geoff asked.

"It's okay with me if it is with her," Adam said.

At her nod, he followed his two daughters and the vet into a room where he set the box atop a metal table. Despite having been reasonably compliant until now, the cat flattened her ears and half growled her disapproval.

"Feisty little thing," Dr. Higgs murmured as he lifted her. "Scrawny but looks healthy. Winnie said you found her out near the lodge?"

"Do you think she belongs to someone already?" Eliza asked worriedly.

"Doubt it. She's lucky to have found nice people. Do you guys know anything about taking care of pets?" he asked them.

"We'll learn!" Eliza promised. "I can check out books at the library and look stuff up on the Internet. And we'll, uh, ask Ms. Pierce for advice. She's smart about animals, right?"

"Very," Dr. Higgs agreed. "She used to work for me. How did you guys meet her?"

"We gave her a ride when her car broke down," Eliza said. She rolled her eyes. "My brother thinks she's a babe."

Dr. Higgs glanced up, startled. Something flashed in his expression, but he apparently thought better of responding. Adam suspected that Brenna's charms hadn't been lost on the man. Adam experienced a twinge of…jealousy.

That's insane. Adam barely knew her.

"This is a case of good timing," Dr. Higgs informed them, his focus back on the cat. "She's not fully mature yet, but she's past kittenhood. A teenager, more or less."

Great. Because Adam needed more teenage drama in his life.

"It's an ideal window of opportunity for getting her spayed," the vet said. "Whenever possible, we like to do it before their first heat but not too far before."

"She's getting sprayed?" Morgan asked.

"Spayed," Adam answered absently. "Do we have to leave her overnight for that?"

"Nope, just bring her in early Monday morning and she should be ready to go home at the end of the day."

Or, more likely, to Brenna's home. Adam found himself curious to see where she lived.

"I can get you some test results in a few minutes, but other than needing to eat more regularly, she looks like she's in good health," Dr. Higgs concluded. "Congratulations. You guys have a new member of the family."

HE'D FIT RIGHT IN with Fred and Josh, Brenna thought with amusement. Her fifteen-year-old companion in the waiting room had asked what the verdict was on her car, then enumerated the qualities she should look for if she decided to buy a new one.

She shook her head. "Don't think that's in my budget anytime soon. The old one's just gonna have to last a little longer."

Geoff pursed his lips. "I know what you mean—no car in *my* budget, either. And I don't even have a hunk of junk to fall back on in the meantime. No offense."

"None taken."

He leaned against the wall behind him, legs stretched out and crossed at the ankles. It seemed like just yesterday that Josh was this age, by turns cocky and endearingly awkward with his impending adulthood.

"Don't get me wrong," Geoff added suddenly. "Dad would probably buy me a car as long as it was reasonably priced and a solid investment. Eliza might act like he's... He's not a bad guy. He's smart, makes good money as a doctor. Some of the music he likes is even kind of cool."

Brenna noted the boy's earnest intensity. Was he used to having to defend his dad, speaking up for him out of habit, or was he specifically trying to impress upon *her* that his dad was a great catch?

"I'm sure he has a lot of good qualities," she said neutrally.

He nodded. "It's just that, even if he helped me with the cost of the car, I need to save up money for gas, insurance, all that stuff."

Tell me about it, kid. She was painfully aware of how quickly "that stuff" added up.

"Mistletoe seems okay, but since we're here for almost a month, I'm not getting to work this summer," he said miserably. "If I had a job, I could start setting aside money for my sixteenth birthday."

"That's a very responsible attitude," she said in praise. A lot of the teens she'd known, her stepbrother included, had spent money as soon as it was handed to them.

Brenna, on the other hand, had hoarded money as a kid—coins she found, a dollar handed to her by one of her mom's boyfriends, even change left under her pillow by the tooth fairy. As if having twelve dollars and sixty-two cents in a purple hippo coin bank would add any security to her life.

"I'm *very* responsible," Geoff said slowly. "A real

hard worker. I mean, my mom hasn't let me get an actual job because she worries it could interfere with classes, but I get great grades. And Mrs. Miller says I do a thorough job cutting her lawn. I do the edging by hand when I'm finished with the grass."

He paused, straightening in his chair. Brenna thought she saw where he was going with this. She wouldn't be able to help him, but she was impressed with his resourcefulness.

"I don't suppose you need any help walking dogs?" he asked, his expression boyishly hopeful.

"Sorry." Technically she *did* need seasonal help—assuming she could generate enough income to pay a second person. But that person would have to be over twenty-one for her company to remain appropriately insured and bonded. "I have special liability insurance because I go in and out of people's homes—like in case something gets broken while I'm there—so I have to follow the age requirements."

They were interrupted by a squeal of delight and Morgan skipping down the hall. She was followed closely by her sister and father.

"Looks like it's time to pick out a name, after all," Adam announced. "And we're gonna need some supplies."

"There's a pet store on Juniper, three blocks over, that allows animals in the store," Brenna said. She had a harness-style cat leash they could borrow; she traveled with a "just in case" plastic storage box stocked with tennis balls, pet leads and assorted treats. "You can follow me there. I've been meaning to drop off more business cards and promotional materials, anyway."

When Kevin joined them, she thanked him without quite meeting his gaze, told him to have a great weekend and excused herself to step outside and return some calls. She liked the good-looking veterinarian, but since their breakup, their conversations had been a touch awkward.

She climbed into her car and had confirmed one schedule change and left a message by the time the Varners piled into their own vehicle. When she met them in front of the pet store, they'd reached a consensus.

"Her name is Ellie," Morgan informed her.

Brenna dutifully assessed the cat that Eliza had cradled against her shoulder. "Yep, she looks like an Ellie! And I have something for her to wear in the store. It's the smallest one I could find, but make sure you keep a good hold on her." She handed Adam the orange kitty harness. His fingers brushed hers, so briefly she shouldn't have even noticed.

But she did.

Chapter Seven

Inside the store Brenna watched the three kids dart in seemingly a dozen different directions. Geoff grabbed a cart while his sisters made a dash for supplies.

"Just the essentials," Adam cautioned them. "Food, a litter box…" Trailing off, he glanced at Brenna questioningly.

"You'll need a cat carrier," she said. "Ellie may have been pretty well behaved for a ride across Mistletoe, but you don't want to drive back to Tennessee with an unsecured cat in the car."

"Definitely not. Carrier, check."

"Maybe a cat bed."

He stopped in front of a multilevel, carpeted kitty condo. "Scratching post?"

"My recommendation would be a scratching pad—inclined corrugated cardboard with some catnip in it. It costs less, it's portable and it's effective for training, redirecting her if she scratches something you'd rather she didn't."

They stopped on an aisle that sold beds and toys. Adam stood back, letting the kids debate colors and laugh at jingly mice. He smiled, but his expression turned sheepish as he faced Brenna. "You probably think I'm a bad parent, bribing my kids to win their affection."

It was odd—and unexpectedly touching—that he might care *what* she thought.

"No," she said softly. "I still remember my first pet." It had been right after her mother walked out on them. Brenna had been in emotional turmoil, but Josh—who'd gone through his parents' divorce, a remarriage and now a sudden abandonment—had been equally overwrought. Fred had taken them to the animal shelter and picked out an exuberant golden retriever puppy they'd named Otis.

For Brenna, that dog had been a godsend. She'd spent far too much of her life, even the relatively quiet and happy times, dreading her mother's next mood swing or capricious life change. And though Fred Pierce was a wonderful man who'd shown her nothing but affectionate welcome, Brenna's ingrained trepidation had remained. If her own *mother* hadn't wanted her, why would a man with no real obligation to her? Otis had shown her unconditional love until the day he'd gone to the great Dog Park in the Sky.

"You okay?" Adam asked.

She blinked, startled to find that her eyes stung. "Sorry, my mind wandered. I was thinking about a golden retriever Josh and I used to have. I realize that, as someone who works with animals, I'm biased, but pets can be a miraculous addition to your life. As long as you don't mind the occasional messes, clawed drapes, getting up to let the dog out at three in the morning and their bringing you something dead to show their love."

Adam's laugh helped put her uncharacteristically sentimental moment behind them. "Wow, when you put it like *that*... No, I do know what you mean. There have been medical studies arguing tangible health benefits of owning pets, like lower blood pressure. A few people even maintain that chances of survival after a heart attack are higher for pet-owners."

"This one?" Morgan asked suddenly, approaching with a small red-and-ivory cat bed.

After exchanging glances with Brenna, who shrugged, Adam nodded. His daughter put the bed into the cart, and the kids rounded the end of the lane into the next aisle. The adults followed at a more leisurely pace, Adam absently rubbing a purring Ellie as they walked.

"So what got you interested in cardiac medicine?" Brenna asked.

"My dad, indirectly. He was my hero when I was young—big, gruff, but with a truly gentle heart. He was an anesthesiologist, used to come home in awe of the surgeries performed at the hospital, the people who'd been healed and the lives that had been saved. I looked up to him, so I guess I decided early that I wanted to be like the doctors *he* looked up to." Adam hesitated, his lips pursed. "Think I fell short of the mark, forgetting somewhere why my dad was such a hero to me in the first place. He was a great father."

"And you don't think you are?" Brenna hadn't meant to ask—the answer, which was none of her business, anyway, was obvious. But the question escaped on a sigh of disbelief. "I realize I barely know you, but I think you're being too hard on yourself."

He flashed her a wan grin. "My ex-wife might disagree."

"Even after this trip? Because I see a man who's trying to sincerely connect with his children. You may have made some mistakes, but who hasn't?"

He was quiet a beat, perhaps mulling over her words. When he spoke again, his tone was lighter, curious. "What about you? You have any mistakes you regret?"

"Me?" The question startled her.

"I'm sorry. That was probably rude to ask."

He looked so chagrined that she blurted, "I make mistakes all the time. Just last week I forgot that a family had changed their alarm code and left my notebook in the car. Thirty seconds after I stepped into their house, the siren was blaring and two cops from the Mistletoe Police Department had to come out.

"The noise nearly gave the poor Chihuahua I was sitting a heart attack. Not to mention, I felt like an idiot in front of several clients, including the next-door neighbor and one of the policemen on call. He has a mynah bird and an African gray parrot."

Her confession might not be emotionally on par with Adam's parental concerns, but his smile was both grateful and sympathetic.

"So, lesson learned," she concluded. "From now on I take my notebook inside even if I've done the assignment a hundred times and feel like I know everything. *Especially* if I feel like I know everything, because those are the times when you forget to notice what's going on around you."

He looked thoughtful. "The same could be said for marriage. I—"

"Dad, we found the food Dr. Higgs recommended," Eliza called from her kneeling position in front of the shelf. "What size bag do we want?"

After that, the kids needed more input and there was less time for Brenna and Adam to talk. Helping the Varners plan for Ellie's care, Brenna found herself back on familiar, neutral territory.

Until Adam pulled out his credit card for the cashier and turned to ask Brenna, "So, should we just follow you to your house now?"

"Dad, is Ms. Pierce trying to lose us?" Geoff asked from the passenger seat.

"No, I'm sure that was an accident," Adam said. *Or a Freudian slip.* Brenna had accelerated at a yellow light just as it became red, stranding Adam behind her. "Look, she's already pulled over on the side of the road to wait for us."

Since they'd agreed earlier that Ellie would stay with Brenna during the remainder of their vacation, he'd assumed he was bringing the cat over. But judging by Brenna's startled expression when he'd asked about going to her house, she had not made the same assumption.

"Actually," she'd explained back at the store, "I don't normally allow customers to drop pets off at my house. It's tougher on the animal. It's more fun for them, more exciting, to 'go for a ride,' which a lot of pets love as much as going for a walk. On the other hand, when their owner leaves them somewhere and they're stuck behind, feeling abandoned…"

She'd trailed off, just for a second, but long enough for Adam to register a fleeting change in her expression.

"Never mind all that," she'd contradicted herself. "Your situation is unusual. Since you guys haven't had time to establish a strong bond yet with Ellie, it makes just as much sense for you to come with me. Help her get settled, visit her a few times while you're in Mistletoe. We don't want her thinking she's my cat at the end of three weeks."

After the intersection, Adam caught up to Brenna and followed her onto a quaint street lined with a hodgepodge of houses—a brick ranch home sat between a two-story log cabin replica and a Cape Cod. It wasn't like modern subdivisions with a grand name, private neighborhood pool and only about three different floor plans alternated between twenty houses.

Brenna's neighborhood—if a single strand of homes could be called that—was eclectic but well kept. Lawns were neatly trimmed, hydrangeas were in bloom and oaks and pear trees provided shady respite from the sweltering heat.

At the curve of the cul-de-sac Brenna pulled her car into the driveway of a stone-faced, cottage-style house. It wasn't big, but it had a generous front yard and what looked to be a huge, fenced-in backyard.

She was out of her car and beside his before he even got his door open. "Sorry about leaving you back there. I don't know what I was thinking." She paused, her lips twisting in a self-deprecating smirk. "I lied. I do know what I was thinking. I had a sudden brain lapse where I thought if I hurried I might have a minute or two to straighten up before you arrived. Which is when it occurred to me that you didn't know how to get here."

He found the explanation endearing. "Don't stress over the house. *We're* the ones imposing." Besides, how messy could her place be? She seemed too brisk and efficient, hardly the type to leave dishes in the sink or toss a towel on the floor.

She went up the front sidewalk, followed by his kids, and Adam felt as if he and the cat were bringing up the rear of a strange little parade. As Brenna unlocked the front door, frenetic barking came from inside.

"Don't worry," she said over her shoulder. "That's my dog, Zoe. She's occasionally noisy, but incredibly friendly."

"Even with cats?" Morgan asked, casting an alarmed glance toward Ellie's new carrier. The feline had flattened herself inside the towel, her ears twitching and her fur puffing with apprehension.

"Absolutely," Brenna assured her. "Zoe and my cat, River, are the best of friends."

Morgan laughed. "River? Cats don't like water."

"Try telling mine that. Now, I'm going in first. You guys give me a sec to put Zoe outside, okay? This will be less chaotic without her in the middle of everything." She disappeared inside, then quickly returned. She ushered them into a living room where two over-stuffed, dark green couches faced each other across a hardwood floor. "Come down the hall, and I'll show you where we can get Ellie's stuff set up."

"It smells awesome in here," Geoff said, inhaling deeply.

Adam had to agree. A blend of spices perfumed the little home, nearly making his stomach rumble.

"Slow-cook pot," Brenna explained. Behind her, he could see into a kitchen. "Since I'm not home much during the day, I throw food in before I leave in the morning."

"What did you fix today?" Eliza asked. Her question made Adam reflect guiltily that it had been a long time since lunch. He was accustomed to skipping a meal here and there if he had a long day of surgery, but the kids needed to eat more regularly.

"Chicken with a citrus marinade," Brenna told his

children, her expression resigned. The three kids had gone so wide-eyed in unspoken longing that Adam was reminded of the famous waif paintings by Margaret Keane, a Tennessee-born artist. "I don't suppose you'd like to stay for dinner?"

"Heck, yeah!" Geoff wasn't shy about accepting the invitation.

Adam was secretly glad for his son's brashness. The polite response was probably to thank her for the offer but insist they couldn't intrude more than they already were. The truth was, Adam had been enjoying her company. He was struck with the realization that it had been ages since he'd spoken to a woman who wasn't a patient, fellow doctor, surgical nurse or his ex-wife. *And her stepbrother claimed* Brenna *had no life?* She wasn't the only one.

"If that's okay with you," Eliza qualified, nudging her brother and jerking her head in Adam's direction.

"Thank you," he told Brenna. "We really appreciate that, really appreciate *everything* you've done for us today."

"You're welcome." Her gaze met his as she smiled, and he felt a funny little twinge of loss when she broke the eye contact. She padded down the hallway, more hardwood covered with a slate-blue runner. Past a set of stairs were two doors on the left—an office and a bathroom—and one on the right. "Here we are, the guest room."

That had no doubt been its original purpose. In here,

the flooring was a tile that looked inexpensive and easy to clean. Instead of a bed and armoire, there was a love seat draped in a fuzzy mauve blanket, two carpeted towers like the kitty condo he'd seen back at the store, a large water bowl, a dog kennel against the far wall and a plastic container filled with chew toys. Up in the windowsill was a small television, and he suspected that Brenna kept on the Animal Planet channel or similar programming for visitors in this room. A cloth mouse dangled from a string looped over the doorknob.

Morgan looked delighted. "It's a playroom for animals!"

Once they were all inside the room, which was barely big enough for five people, Brenna closed the door. "Go ahead, put Ellie down. We'll let her explore for a minute. Can one of you go get her litter-box supplies?"

Adam shot his children a pointed glance. "I seem to recall lots of promises in the car about taking responsibility for your new pet?"

He got a trio of quick nods, and all three children started toward the bedroom door.

"Be careful not to let Brenna's cat outside," he warned.

"Oh, she spends her day on the screened-in sunporch," Brenna said. "We'll let her in soon."

The kids slid through a partially open door while Ellie tiptoed around her new surroundings.

Adam's conscience prompted him to ask, "You're *sure* it's okay if we stay for dinner?"

"As long as no one looks too closely at any of the

furniture. I vacuum a lot to keep up with the animal hair, but I don't spend a lot of time dusting. Just one of those things I unintentionally let slide because no one ever comes over."

"Not even Josh? Or…a boyfriend?" He'd wondered since first seeing her yesterday if she was single. Though her stepbrother had all but confirmed it, Adam found that he wanted to hear it straight from her lips.

"Not for a long time," she admitted. "Not since Kevin."

"Dr. Higgs?" So he hadn't been imagining the veterinarian's reaction to her.

"Yeah. We dated for a while, but we wanted different things. My fault, probably. When you're starting your own company, it can be pretty all-consuming. I barely had time and energy left over for myself, much less enough for another person."

"Being a surgeon is a bit like that," he commiserated. "From what little I saw on our walk-through, your house looks clean to me. And you smiled and waved at about a dozen people in the Diner. You've been working all day, and yet still managed to have a dinner waiting for you when you got home. I envy your balance."

"Balance?" She laughed. "You should come to Sunday dinner and tell my family that. They'd laugh you out of the house. You heard what Josh said about me last night."

"Yes, but he's wrong," Adam said, questioning his

own vested interest. In a few weeks he'd be gone from Mistletoe, so what did it matter whether Brenna was able to balance romance in her busy schedule?

She arched an eyebrow. "He's known me most of my life. You've only known me two days."

"Still." He smiled. "It's always best to get a second opinion."

IF ANYONE HAD told Adam that during his family vacation, he'd be having dinner two nights in a row with the same beautiful woman, he would have assumed feverish delirium and checked the speaker's temperature. Or possibly have ordered a CAT scan.

Yet here he was in Brenna's kitchen, instructing his kids to scrub in for supper. Since there were only four chairs at the oval table in her kitchen, she'd gone to grab the desk chair from her office. He asked Morgan to sit on the side closest to the wall since it was easiest for her to squeeze in; while he filled glasses with ice cubes, Geoff and Eliza seated themselves at either end. When Brenna returned, rolling the padded office chair up to the oblong table, Adam realized he'd be sitting next to her. Closely.

As tantalizing as the food smelled, when he was in such close proximity to Brenna, he didn't notice the aromas of garlic or orange. Instead, it seemed as if he could only breathe in the heady smell of her, some kind of vanilla-based mixture that was sweet without being flowery or cloying. Her lotion or shampoo, maybe?

Whatever it was, he liked it a lot. Much like Brenna herself, it was sexy without being blatantly obvious.

As dinner progressed, she finally struck a casual balance between trying hard—apologizing for any imagined housekeeping deficiencies, chatting a mile a minute about the town's amenities—and holding herself courteously aloof, as he'd sensed her doing when they first arrived at the vet's office. She regaled them with anecdotes about River, a long-haired tortoiseshell Manx with no tail. Unlike any other cat Adam knew, River would play fetch and loved to annoy the dog by taking off with Zoe's smaller toys and hiding them in hard-to-reach places. As a child, Adam hadn't owned a cat, but there'd been two big dogs in his home.

Smiling over long-forgotten memories, Adam recounted how their family German shepherd had been afraid of the yappy little poodle next door, and told the story of a dinner party that had been ruined when the pork roast that had been cooling on a counter disappeared entirely.

"Until that evening, I didn't realize Mom even *knew* any bad words," Adam reminisced. His parents were retired near Crossville now and owned a medium-size mutt they'd brought with them in February when they visited for Geoff's birthday.

Adam frowned when he realized he hadn't seen them since then—and he'd barely spent any time with them during that visit because one of his repeat patients had suffered a massive pulmonary embolism that week. His parents were generally more understanding about the demands of his career than his children, but the fact remained that Adam was struggling to prioritize between saving other people's lives and being there for the people in his own life.

After dinner the kids checked on Ellie, then decided to take advantage of the beautiful summer weather by playing Frisbee in the backyard with Zoe.

"I could call them back in," Adam offered, carrying three plates and a half-empty glass, "and get them to help us with dishes."

Brenna shook her head. "Nah, we'd just be tripping over one another in this tiny kitchen. As it is, you and I keep…"

Bumping? Brushing against each other? He'd noticed. And he liked it. While he didn't deliberately collide with her—he had more maturity than Geoff, for pity's sake—he didn't go out of his way to step aside if she was passing him, either.

"Anyway." She swallowed. "Border collies are active dogs. It's good they're giving Zoe the extra playtime and exercise since I've been gone a lot this week."

"Are you all done for the day?" he asked, trying not to stare as she bent over to wipe the far side of the table. She had an amazing figure. It seemed as if, over the past few years, he'd fallen into the implausible habit of thinking about the human form in only clinical terms. Brenna's body was more art than science.

"Nope." When she answered him, he struggled momentarily to remember what his question had been. "I'll do about an hour of office work, then head back out to put some dogs in for the night. Not everyone has doggie doors installed, and there are a lot of reasons not to leave dogs out all night—weather, increased barking and, for the smaller dogs, the threat of coyotes."

"So how did you come to work with animals?" he asked. "It sounds great in theory—be your own boss, play with cute puppies—but the reality seems pretty difficult.

"It's rewarding, mostly. I've loved animals ever since I was a little girl, and as I mentioned last night, the nine-to-five thing just wasn't for me."

"Not enough working hours in the day?" he teased.

She grinned over her shoulder. "It was more the corporate culture, office politics. As it turns out, I apparently don't play well with others."

In her flippant response, she was selling herself short. He didn't know much about pet-sitting, but he knew what it was like to work with various personality types. His patients had all kinds of quirks and preferences, but they needed him. Brenna had made it sound as if she was actively striving to grow her business, which must require good word of mouth, which meant she had to be careful to cater to her clients. Even if one was being a pain in the butt.

"Do you like the majority of the people you work for?" he wanted to know.

She tossed her dishcloth into the sink. "Yeah. I appreciate every one of them—even the ones who change their pet's diet or medication and forget to tell me, or the ones who have nanny-cams installed every ten inches and make me feel like I'm stuck in my own reality television show. Obviously I couldn't do this for a living without my customers, but it's more than that.

"I'm grateful to them for…making me part of their lives." She winced. "Well, that sounded corny as hell."

Adam smiled, charmed equally by the personal revelation and her subsequent cranky reaction.

Abruptly she changed the subject. "Other than getting her a cat, which should qualify you as the most beloved parent in all of Mistletoe, have you figured out what you're going to do for Morgan's birthday?"

"No." Finished with the dishes, he leaned against the counter. "I'm open to suggestions."

"Earlier today I remembered something my stepmother did once. She treated me to a girlie day at the local spa. Mani, pedi, sparkly lipstick. At Morgan's age, she might get a kick out of being treated like a princess. Eliza could do it with her, but I guess that leaves you and Geoff out in the cold."

"It might work," Adam said slowly. With three kids, it was difficult to get one-on-one time with each. Maybe he and Geoff could have some time to chat while the girls enjoyed an hour or two of glamour. And it was the type of thing that would be a surprise— people expected moms to come up with beauty-day ideas, not fathers.

"So, your dad married Josh's mom?" he asked. If

Brenna and her father were close, perhaps she could give him some insight into improving his relationship with Eliza.

"No."

"But…" Hadn't she said Josh was her stepbrother? And she mentioned a stepmother.

Brenna turned to the window overlooking that backyard. "I hate to break up the kids' fun, but I really do have some computer work I should get to."

"Of course, sorry." The last thing he'd wanted was to overstay his welcome. "I should have herded them inside sooner, instead of sticking around to shoot the bull."

"I've never liked that saying," Brenna admonished with mock affront. "But at least it's not as bad as 'more than one way to skin a cat.' What kind of monster came up with that?" She gave an exaggerated shudder.

Was the silly banter her way of softening the impression that she was kicking them out?

"From here on out, only metaphors in which no animals are harmed," he promised solemnly. "Where do you stand on 'raining cats and dogs'?"

Her lips twitched as she tried to keep her expression deadpan. "It depends. Are they wearing protective gear?" At the last moment, her suppressed smile broke free, making her truly beautiful, and it was as if something inside Adam had been liberated, too.

Without conscious, rational thought, he leaned forward and kissed her.

At first it was only the feather-light contact of his

mouth against her smile, but even that sent a jolt straight through him and down to his toes. He nipped at her bottom lip, grazing his tongue over her, nearly overcome with the urge to haul her closer, frame her face in his hands and kiss her deeply. *I want her.* Wanted her smiles, her playful conversation, her more serious observations about life and her delectable body.

Stunned at the intensity of his reaction, he righted himself. "I…" Should apologize, yet he couldn't bring himself to say he was sorry. How could he pretend to regret the kiss when what he really wanted was to do it again? Soon. *Thoroughly.*

"Should go," she supplied tremulously, as if unsure of her own words. Her clear green eyes were startled. But did they also reflect back something more? "You should get going."

"Right." His feet wouldn't move.

They stood there for a heartbeat that felt like a lifetime, staring at each other.

He cleared his throat. "I'll round up my kids."

She nodded, bemused.

Neither of them said anything else, but when he got to the back door, he couldn't resist looking over his shoulder at her. She remained in the same spot, motionless. Except that she'd pressed her fingers to her lips.

As he stepped through the doorway, a whisper of sound followed him. He thought it might have been *Wow.*

Chapter Eight

"Hey, sis." Josh opened the front door wider to let Brenna past, but rather than flash one of his customary smiles, he scowled with concern. "Are you getting enough sleep?"

"Not even close," she admitted with a wan smile. "So stop badgering me to go out with Nick Zeth or J. C. Delgorio or whoever you're trying to fix me up with next and just let me stay home so I can go to bed early."

Little does my brother know. She didn't need his help finding a man to stir her interest—she'd been kissing just such a man in her kitchen two nights ago!

Josh narrowed his eyes. "What?"

"I didn't say anything."

"No, but you were thinking something. I could smell the smoke."

"Ha ha." She poked him in the shoulder. "You're hilarious. You ever think about taking that act on the road…far, far from Mistletoe?"

Natalie appeared behind him in the doorway that led from the foyer into the dining room where they'd all be eating. "Josh, are you giving your sister a hard time?"

"Nah, we were just chatting. Apparently she's too tired to date."

Maggie poked her head around the corner, wiping flour-dusted hands on her apron. No doubt she'd just put one of her wonderful pies in the oven. "Date? Brenna, honey, did you go on a date this weekend?"

"What can I help with?" Brenna asked, effectively sidestepping the issue of romance.

For a whole twenty-three minutes.

As Fred passed the barbecued chicken to Brenna, he asked, "Know who I saw at Waide Supply?"

Brenna hazarded a guess. "One of the Waides?" Zachariah and his wife had owned the hardware and feed store for years, but it was mostly run these days by David Waide and his sister, Arianne.

"No, Gabriel Sloan, buying some equipment. He's still single, isn't he?"

At the mention of the man with the semi-infamous past, Maggie choked on her dilled cucumber and tomato salad. "Gabe Sloan? But he—"

"Don't you think there comes a time when we all have to let go of the past and move forward?" Fred wasn't looking at his wife as he asked the question, but his stepdaughter.

I am moving forward! She was building her own

company, establishing real roots in the community, creating the stability she'd always craved.

Fred heaved a sigh. "I just want to see you happy, Bren. I've gone it alone and I've been in love. It makes a world of difference."

"Well, when I can find a man as loyal as my dog, I'll think about it," she joked. "Let's face it, Zoe would drag my unconscious body out of a burning building, while half the men in the world can't even manage to call when they say they will."

Natalie laughed, but tried to disguise it as a cough when Josh sent her a hurt look.

"Oh, honey." Maggie's expression was so maternal and concerned that it twisted something in Brenna sideways. "That's not why you broke up with Kevin, is it, because you questioned his loyalty?"

"No, I wasn't speaking literally," Brenna said with a sigh. *For starters,* he *broke up with* me. "I just… So, Nat, how's the flower business?"

Giving her a sympathetic glance, Natalie began telling them all about a wedding she was doing next weekend and the bride's various meltdowns so far. Then there was a wedding scheduled for the Fourth of July in which the bride had gone wholeheartedly with the red-white-and-blue theme. Not only in the flowers, but in gowns—her two bridesmaids would be wearing red-and-blue dresses.

Brenna listened with half an ear. Maggie's question about Kevin had reminded her of one of the last things he'd said before correctly deciding they were not meant to be. He'd been in Intense Discussion mode.

"It must have killed you when your mother left," he'd said.

"Not so much." She'd tried to joke away old pains. "Here I am, still alive."

"Poor Brenna." He'd brushed his hand over her hair soothingly. "Is that why you're so aloof? Metaphorically leaving people before they can leave you."

And about a week later, Kevin had left her.

Which was for the best, but he'd had a point. If she ever hoped to find the happiness Fred and Maggie shared, the kind that Josh and Natalie aspired to, she would have to get better at opening up to people.

Her mind flitted back to Adam. What would it be like if she let herself get involved, just on a short-term basis, with someone she already *knew* was leaving? It wasn't as if she would have to wonder in the back of her mind when it would all end. The idea was morbidly appealing. It replaced chance and romantic whim with a modicum of control and certainty.

Lost in thought, she almost missed it when Josh suddenly said, "I saw the Varner family at the lodge this morning."

Brenna's gaze flew to his face, searching for any sign of knowing smugness. Had Josh guessed that she was thinking about Adam? Had he somehow sensed any of the attraction she felt for the doctor?

"I talked to them as they were headed out tubing."

He smiled. "That Morgan is one cute kid. Says she's turning five this week."

"Friday," Brenna provided reflexively.

Maggie raised her eyebrows. "Who are the Varners? I can't place the name."

"I'm pet-sitting for them while they're on vacation at the lodge," Brenna said. They would meet her at the vet clinic in the morning when she dropped off Ellie for her procedure. Kevin would give Adam a call after the operation to let him know how the little cat was recuperating.

"The Varners are those tourists from Tennessee," Josh clarified. "Remember? The surgeon who picked up Brenna? Adam really wants to take his two oldest rafting, but Morgan's too young. Nat, I told him I'd see if you might be willing to babysit."

Natalie bit her lip. "I don't know. I mean, I'd love to, that's not a question, but the shortest trip you do is almost four hours. I've got multiple weddings and receptions coming up, not to mention the float for the Independence Day parade."

Brenna found herself hoping that Josh hadn't made his babysitting offer within earshot of the kids. It sounded as if there had been past occasions when they'd had their hopes dashed when it came to time with their father, and she didn't want her stepbrother indirectly contributing to that.

After dinner Fred said he wanted to check scores before dessert and, predictably, fell asleep in his recliner three and a half minutes later. Maggie shooed Josh and Natalie out the door the second they'd finished their pie so they wouldn't miss the late movie they'd been planning to see.

"I'm more than willing to clear the table by myself," Maggie assured them. "It's worth it, getting to spend the evening with you all."

Brenna hesitated. She could spare a tiny bit of time before starting her "good night" visits; the Turners lived over in this neck of the woods, anyway.

"I'll help with the dishes," she told Maggie. When the offer reminded her of Adam—and the steamy moment they'd shared in her kitchen—she nearly groaned. It was a bad sign when menial housework got you worked up over a guy.

Maggie looked taken aback. "Well, thank you, honey. I figured after the conversation earlier, you'd beat feet to get out of here."

"Which conversation?" Brenna asked as she collected all the linen napkins for the laundry. "Oh, you mean the one where Fred has stooped to randomly pawning me off on any single man who crosses his path? I've forgotten all about it."

"Sorry if we put you on the spot," Maggie said sheepishly. "We're just…"

"Trying to be my family." And family members looked out for one another, even if it came in the form of unsolicited dating advice. "Maggie Pierce, you're a hell of a good mother."

For a second Maggie didn't react. She went from frozen to blinking rapidly, tears welling up in her eyes. "I...I need to put these away in the fridge." She blindly grabbed two containers off the dining-room table, one of which was empty.

Brenna gave her a second of privacy, then followed her into the kitchen with a stack of plates. Maggie had one arm braced against the kitchen counter and was wiping her eyes with her free hand.

"You okay?" Brenna asked softly. Jeez, no wonder she avoided the touchy-feely stuff as a rule. She hadn't meant to make Maggie feel bad.

"I apologize for..." Maggie fluttered her hand in a vague gesture. "You just caught me off guard."

If kind words from Brenna were startling enough to elicit an emotional meltdown, then she was the worst stepdaughter ever.

Abashed, she asked, "You *do* know that I...love you, right?" The words didn't come easily, hadn't for decades, but that didn't mean the feeling behind them was absent.

"Oh, honey." Maggie reached out to squeeze Brenna's hand. "I do know. You've never wanted to talk about your mom—"

"I still don't," Brenna said quickly.

"But I hope you know I love you like my own daughter."

Even though Brenna had been quietly prickly in the beginning about accepting that love. Oh, she'd never been as outwardly bratty as Eliza—she hadn't been that brave—but scared and scarred, she couldn't have made it easier for the older woman, either.

"Josh mentioned the Varner family?" Brenna began. She enthusiastically scrubbed dishes, glad to have something physical to do—and an excuse not to meet Maggie's eye. "A divorced man and his three kids. I think watching him interact with them is part of what made me realize how much I appreciate you. He's worried he's not doing a good-enough job—"

"All parents feel that way," Maggie empathized.

"—but he's so patient with them, trying so hard to reach out to them. He may not see it as objectively as I do, but he's a great kisser."

It wasn't until Maggie's jaw dropped that Brenna realized what she'd said.

"F-father. I meant he's a great father."

Maggie raised her eyebrows expectantly.

"He really is great. With them. A very committed dad."

Still silent, Maggie shifted her weight.

Brenna tossed her hands up in defeat. "Oh, all right, *and* he's a great kisser. Judging from the single, solitary peck I have to go by."

Maggie beamed at her. "And will you be kissing him again?"

"No!" Maybe. *I sure hope so.*

Chapter Nine

Adam was so out of practice with women that for one insane instant he actually considered seeking the advice of his fifteen-year-old son. *So, Geoff, tell me about the first time you kissed your girlfriend. Was it awkward the next time you saw her? Did you mention it or just play it cool?*

Resisting the urge to bang his head on the steering wheel, Adam cranked up the music in the SUV to drown out his own asinine thoughts. All too soon, they'd reached the shopping center where Dr. Higgs practiced. It was very early in the day—technically the office didn't even open for another half hour, but Dr. Higgs had explained that when the visit was surgical, he preferred to get an animal checked in before the lobby got hectic. It reminded Adam of the times he'd told a patient they needed to report to the hospital by 6 a.m. for pre-op. Most people agreed that was preferable to waiting half a day when they weren't allowed to put anything in their stomachs after midnight.

Brenna could have gone in the clinic, but as she had last time, she was waiting out at her car. With the two of them meeting here in a deserted lot, this felt almost like a clandestine encounter. Until he parked and his kids all began chattering at once, unbuckling their seat belts and practically tripping over themselves in their haste to see Ellie and Brenna.

Adam lagged behind, studying her. She wore a black leather headband today, securing her coppery hair out of her face. She had on black-and-red athletic shorts and a white T-shirt emblazoned with her company logo. There was nothing sexy or glamorous about her appearance, but damn, he wanted to kiss her again.

She shaded her eyes against the sun. "Morning."

"Hi. Thanks for meeting us here. Are you sure you want to pick Ellie up this afternoon? If you're busy with other animals, I can come get her. We could meet back at your place," he suggested impulsively. "The kids and I could bring dinner. We owe you."

He was almost certain she would say no—after all, she'd made it clear how crowded her work schedule was. And he still wasn't one hundred percent sure how she'd felt about his kissing her.

She nibbled indecisively at her lower lip, and it took real effort for him to tear his gaze away from her mouth. "Why not?" she finally said. "It might take some minor rearranging, but…I guess I have to eat sometime, right?"

The words might not have been the most enthusiastic encouragement a man ever received, but her casual statement was belied by the smile she gave him. Bright, appreciative and a touch mischievous. A smile like that could make a man weak in the knees.

"Brenna!" Morgan tugged at the hem of the woman's shorts. "I made a card for Ellie. Wanna see?"

"Of course." Holding Adam's gaze for just a moment longer, the pet-sitter knelt and turned to give his daughter her undivided attention. They talked for a few seconds about how Ellie would be a bit groggy afterward, but wouldn't feel any pain during the procedure.

"You guys can come visit her tonight," Brenna said, brushing Morgan's hair away from her face. "But she probably won't feel like playing. Zoe, on the other hand, will be *thrilled* to see you. Think you could do me a favor and play some more Frisbee with her?"

Morgan brightened. "That would be so fun!"

"Great. Then I'll see you later." Having delivered the cat and agreeing that Adam would be the one picking her up, Brenna turned to go. She looked astonished when Morgan threw her arms around her legs in an impromptu hug.

Adam was surprised, too. Morgan was sweet-natured, but he'd never seen her warm up to someone this quickly. Heck, even with him she'd been timid on occasion, shy to tell him about her day. He'd picked her up at preschool once and when another child asked who he was, Morgan had said, "That's Dr. Daddy." Yet there was no sense of that formality or hesitation with Brenna.

A fact that did not escape his other children's notice. Eliza and Geoff exchanged meaningful glances, then turned to him as if to ask half-a-dozen simultaneous, silent questions. He sighed. For an extremely educated man with fifteen years of parenting experience, Dr. Daddy had surprisingly few answers.

"MORE THAN PUPPY LOVE, this is Brenna."

"Hey. It's Adam."

Inexplicably, Brenna was reminded of a day she'd gone with Fred and Josh to Kerrigan Farms and they'd helped make real old-fashioned ice cream—the kind you had to hand-crank. She recalled drizzling rich, golden caramel—her favorite topping—over a bowl of vanilla. Adam's voice sounded the way that sweet liquid caramel had looked. Warm, addictive, delicious. If she hadn't been driving her car, she would have closed her eyes to better savor listening to him.

"Brenna? You going through an area with bad cell reception?"

"N-no, I can hear you perfectly." *I'm apparently suffering delayed heatstroke because my brain has turned to mush, but nothing wrong with my hearing.* "Are you calling with a status report on Ellie?"

"Dr. Higgs said she's doing great, and we can pick her up in about an hour. He even spoke to Morgan when he called."

Brenna smiled at that. "Sounds like Kevin. So where are you now?"

"We've been lazing by the pool." Adam lowered his voice. "Which was incredibly peaceful until about ten minutes ago."

"Why? What happened then?"

"Changing of the guards," he snarled. So much for the smooth, dreamy caramel voice.

She laughed. "Have you guys jetted off to Buckingham Palace without letting me know?"

"Lifeguards," he said succinctly. Beneath his breath, he added, "Punk."

"Problem?"

"Yes. Boys are my problem. They're inconsiderate, inconsistent and only out for One Thing," he complained in a bitter undertone. "The other day, one of these horrid creatures caught my daughter's eye."

"I see." Brenna tried not to laugh at his expense. "So is she over there flirting with him?"

She recalled that, in her teens, Fred had been so mortified at the thought of her dating, she'd more or less avoided the situation until college. *And now he's practically going through the phone book trying to find me a guy.* She didn't have the heart to tell Adam that parenting a daughter would probably never get any easier.

"The other day, he was flirting with Eliza. Who is way too young for him, I might add. But now he has the colossal nerve to stand there in plain sight flirting with some fourteen- or fifteen-year-old girl whose parents obviously lack the funds to buy her the *whole* bathing suit."

"You're cute when you rant."

That stopped him cold. "Cute? I'm not sure how I feel about that."

"If it helps, I meant it in a good way."

"Yeah?" He sounded positively cheerful now, the evil lifeguard forgotten. "Well, I think you're cute, too. And by 'cute,' I mean incredibly sexy."

Sexy? Her mouth fell open. She couldn't recall the last time a man had called her that. "Thank you."

The way he'd looked at her the other night, the way he'd confidently kissed her with no warning—that had all been sexy. At the time she just hadn't been sure she wanted to act on the latent desires he provoked. Now that she'd had a couple of days to think about it…

"Adam?"

"I'm listening," he said.

"About that k—"

"Oh, hell," he interrupted. "I gotta go. My little girl's crying."

She knew he meant Eliza and not Morgan. "Go. I'll see you tonight."

Though she applauded his efforts to comfort his daughter, the aborted conversation was a reminder that an uncomplicated summer fling with a single dad was probably an oxymoron. How could anything remain uncomplicated when kids were involved? Common sense settled over her like an itchy wool blanket. She didn't want to interfere in the Varners' family time, and she didn't want to set a controversial example for those kids. It was better that she and Adam remain platonic and that she didn't think of him as anything more than a customer she liked and respected. In fact, it would probably be for the best that she stopped thinking about him entirely.

Yes, that was definitely what she would do. Put him out of her mind.

How hard could that be?

IT WAS WEIRD to come home to someone besides a dog and cat who wanted to be fed.

When Brenna pulled into her driveway, the Varners had already parked under the carport and gone inside. Adam had called her back earlier to find out if she had any food allergies or vehement preferences on what she wanted to eat. It had occurred to her that since her schedule was made up more of rough estimates than exact times, she should tell him where the spare key was hidden in the backyard. She warned him that Zoe would definitely come through the doggie door to investigate his presence. Since the border collie had already given the Varners her canine stamp of approval, however, the worst threat she posed was trying to lick one of them in the face.

Brenna had hesitated over telling him how to get into the house—it felt bizarrely personal to think of Adam and his three kids under her roof, amid her stuff, when she wasn't there—but then she'd realized what a hypocrite she was being. After all, people let *her* into the privacy of their homes every day!

She opened the front door and did a double take. The enticing food smell wasn't entirely unfamiliar, but the sounds of Adam calling out hello, Morgan scurrying to come greet her and Geoff laughing at some antic of Zoe's… It was as if Brenna had turned the knob and accidentally walked into someone else's life, instead of her own. She blinked, her stepfather's words coming back to her: *I've gone it alone, and I've been in love. It makes a world of difference.*

"Brenna! I drew you a picture," Morgan said. "It's on your fridge. Wanna see?"

They passed through the living room, where Geoff and Zoe were playing tug-of-war with a stuffed toy.

"Ellie's sleeping in the kitty den," Morgan explained. "If she feels better tomorrow, will you play with her for us?"

"Absolutely," Brenna promised.

They'd reached the kitchen, where Adam was popping open takeout containers and pouring food into bowls. The scene was so domestic that she felt she should kiss him on the cheek and ask him about his day. *Platonic,* she reminded herself. No kissing on the cheek or anywhere else.

"We had a craving for Chinese," he said. "Please tell me Mistletoe has decent mu shu pork."

"There is no bad food in Mistletoe," she promised. "Well, except for a couple of ill-advised recipes I tried. But most of my dinner guests survived those and, with therapy and time, even went on to live normal lives."

Morgan wrinkled her nose. "You're funny."

Choosing to take that as a compliment, Brenna glanced around. "Where's Eliza?"

Adam jerked his head toward the sunporch adjacent to the kitchen. Brenna moved closer for a better look through the window, sidestepping Morgan as the little girl rejoined Zoe and Geoff in the living room. Seated on a white-wicker padded bench, Eliza had River in her lap and was singing along mournfully to a tune from her iPod.

"Ah. The continuing saga of boy troubles?" Brenna asked.

"Yeah." Adam leaned in to peer over her shoulder and check on his daughter. Brenna's body heated at his nearness. He smelled like outdoors and sunshine. And he was close enough that she heard his breathing quicken.

Maybe she should fill *him* in on the platonic plan.

She ducked away from him, gesturing at the window. "You want me to go talk to her?"

He gnawed at the inside of his cheek. "Can you talk to her about it without letting her know I told you anything?"

She thought it over. "Can do." Whether it would actually *help* was a different story, but it seemed like a fitting homage to Maggie and all the times she'd tried to bridge the natural gap between her and Brenna. Plus, it put space between Brenna and Adam.

Even without those reasons, though, she admitted

to herself that she probably would have felt compelled
to reach out to the girl. Unexpectedly Adam Varner and
his entire family were getting under Brenna's skin in
a remarkably short period. They were tugging at heart-
strings normally reserved for litters of puppies and
stray kittens in the rain.

It was ironic that Dr. Varner helped people im-
prove their heart function. Because the more time she
spent in his company, the more erratically her heart
seemed to behave.

"HEY." BECAUSE OF the iPod, Brenna spoke louder
than she normally would. "Mind if I join you for a
few minutes?"

Sniffling, the girl averted her face. "It's your house."

"That doesn't really answer the question." Brenna
stood in front of the girl, scratching River under her
chin. "Looks like you've made a new friend here."

It had been the wrong thing to say.

"I don't need *new* friends. I need my real ones, back
home! They're the people I want to talk to. Or even my
mom. Do you know how gross it is to talk to a dad
about boys?"

"Can't say that I do. I never got up the courage to
try." She wasn't sure who it would have psychologi-
cally scarred more, her or Fred. The man loved her, no
question of that, but when it came to "female matters,"
he'd invariably punted her in Maggie's direction. "It
just seemed too awkward."

Eliza nodded repeatedly. "It is. Trust me. And what does he know, anyway?"

"Cut him some slack, Eliza. Your dad's an intelligent guy, and he cares about you."

"That doesn't make him an expert on dating. He hasn't had a girlfriend since my mom."

Really? *Women in Knoxville don't know what they're missing.* Of course, Brenna doubted he kept his children posted on the particulars of his love life, so it was possible he was more experienced than they realized. For instance, she was certain they didn't know about that kiss the other night—and she planned to keep it that way.

"What about you?" Eliza demanded suddenly. "You're probably smarter about romance than him. Do you date often?"

Brenna guffawed. "Even less than your dad, actually."

"But you're pretty. And you have…" Eliza didn't finish her sentence, but she glanced meaningfully in the vicinity of Brenna's chest. "My friend Dee says that's all a girl needs to attract a guy."

There were so many things wrong with that statement—not that it was completely without truth—Brenna didn't know where to start. "Those guys aren't really worth attracting."

"What kind *are?*"

"Scoot over." It would be a snug fit, but the bench could accommodate both of them. Since it looked as if Brenna might need a few minutes to come up with answers, she preferred to get off her feet. "Okay. Boys are a pain in the you-know-what."

Eliza giggled. *Progress.*

"But some of them are at least worth the trouble. Hold out for one of those, one who respects you, who's courteous. He should be honest with you and listen when you talk. He needs to recognize your boundaries and not push you to do anything you aren't comfortable with."

"I *know* this part," Eliza said, rolling her eyes.

"All right. Well, since you should also listen when *he* talks, it helps if you have some common interests. And if he's funny."

The girl frowned. "Bobby likes to talk mostly about Camaros and himself. Hearing about him was interesting at first, but…"

"Did he ever ask about you?"

"Not really."

"Find a guy who does. But there's no hurry," she stipulated.

That earned her another eye roll, but Eliza's expression was much brighter than it had been. She set River aside and got to her feet. "Is dinner almost ready? I think I'm hungry."

Brenna figured that doing a victory dance would be inappropriate—or make her look like an idiot, at any rate—but the impulse was there. While she wasn't naive enough to think that Eliza would go forth and never suffer boy troubles again, helping the adolescent past this hiccup was far more rewarding than she could have predicted.

At the door leading back into the main house, Eliza paused. "What about you, Ms. Pierce? Is the reason you don't date much because you're still holding out? You haven't found a guy who's funny and respectful and a good listener?"

Brenna blinked, surprised to find herself the topic of conversation again. "Oh. I've been lucky enough to find a couple of guys who fit that description, but none of them were quite... I don't have that much time to date. I work a lot."

Eliza's mouth thinned. "Like my father." She clearly didn't mean it as a compliment.

"He does an important job." She experienced an uncharacteristically self-conscious moment when she compared their occupations. Scooping kitty litter and sprinkling fish flakes into an aquarium sounded a bit less impressive.

"People are important, too." Eliza crossed her arms over her chest, narrowing her eyes suspiciously. "Maybe you aren't as smart about relationships as I thought."

Chapter Ten

Wanting to ensure that he didn't undo everything his kids had learned about good manners in three weeks, Adam made it clear that they were responsible for the dishes this time. Of course, that only consisted of throwing empty containers in the garbage and scrubbing five plates.

"Before we go, can we play with River and Zoe for just a few minutes?" Morgan begged. The three of them were endlessly entertained by the way the cat chased after toys just like the dog.

He deferred to Brenna, glancing her way with raised eyebrows.

"Ten minutes," she said.

Not wanting to waste any of that, the kids disappeared into the backyard with a stampede of footsteps and the back door banging shut.

He'd been dying to know how her conversation with Eliza went—was the girl difficult with all adults, or was it just him?—but hadn't been able to get specifics until now. "So—"

"Do you want coffee?" Brenna asked brightly. "I could make us some coffee."

"Didn't we just give the kids a ten-minute warning?" He was pretty sure they couldn't brew and subsequently chug a hot beverage in that amount of time. Was this Brenna's way of demonstrating that she was reluctant for their evening to end?

"Right." She cast rather desperate looks about her small kitchen. "It's really too hot for coffee, anyway. What we need is something cold. Ice-cream floats?"

"Brenna, are you trying to find something to do because you're…nervous? About being alone with me?" If that was the case, should he be flattered or appalled? He didn't want to scare her.

She took a deep breath, shoving her hands into the pockets of her shorts. "You caught me. I am a little apprehensive that…"

"That I might kiss you again?" *Nice going, Varner. You've driven the woman to an anxiety attack.*

Brenna's gaze collided with his. "No, that I might kiss you."

Her words, delivered with such artless sensuality, seared him. "I would be okay with that. Just so you know."

She laughed, but it had a hoarse, husky edge to it. "But would your kids be okay with it?"

He wanted to say that they were irrelevant to the discussion at hand, but he was a father—his children were *never* irrelevant. And he guiltily recalled the questions he'd fielded on their very first day in Mistletoe, when he'd all but promised them he wouldn't seek out any romantic connections while they were here. Fresh on the heels of Sara's marriage, it was natural for the kids to be curious about his dating. Morgan already adored Brenna; it would be dangerous to encourage that. Eliza, on the other hand, was thawing toward him bit by bit and would no doubt freeze up in betrayed disapproval if he got too close to Brenna in their limited time together.

And it would be limited. He hadn't been able to retain a strong relationship with his own family *who lived under the same roof* as him. He didn't delude himself that he was cut out for the rigors of a long-distance relationship. Not with his job and three children who deserved as much time as he could give them.

Frustrated, he plowed a hand through his hair. "I wish things were different."

"Oh, you have no idea how many times I've had reason to think that." She gave him a bittersweet smile. "For what it's worth, I'm glad you kissed me the other day. I just don't think it's a good idea…"

"I agree." In practice, if not in spirit.

Silence descended on them.

Brenna rocked back on her heels. "If we're gonna spend the next five minutes in painful awkwardness, we might as well get comfortable. Want to join me in the living room?"

They both sat on the same sofa, but curled up at opposite ends with an entire upholstered cushion separating them. Even the strictest chaperone would approve. Adam tried not to be depressed.

"Did I tell you that I looked into that idea you had for Morgan's party, at a salon? I even tested it by asking if she likes to have her nails done."

"And?"

"She was practically giddy about the idea. There aren't many places here in town, but I called all of them. The only stumbling block is that I can't drop the girls off. One woman said she might accept a twelve-year-old being there alone, but no way would she be comfortable taking responsibility for two kids, especially when one is so young."

"You should go with them," Brenna said.

He couldn't tell if she was kidding or not.

"Ask for Linda at Beautiful Day," Brenna added, wiggling her fingers. "She gives a great hand massage. I'm not suggesting you get sparkly decals—"

He shot her a look that let her know what he thought of *that* possibility.

"—but you could get your nails, I don't know, buffed or something."

Eliza and Morgan would probably find that hysterically funny. It didn't mesh with his original idea of making use of one-on-one time with Geoff, but why not? "I guess Geoff's mature enough to read in the waiting area. Because there's no way he'll agree to participate." Adam grinned, imagining how his teenager would react to such a suggestion.

Tilting her head back, Brenna addressed the ceiling. "I can't believe I'm about to say this… What if I hired Geoff for the afternoon?"

"What?"

She shrugged. "He might have mentioned something about wanting to earn cash this summer. Take Morgan and Eliza out to a daddy-daughter lunch. If there's one thing I've noticed about Geoff, it's that he isn't picky about food. He can eat a couple of hot dogs here. I'll pay him for a few hours of filing and light office work while the girls get their mani-pedis.

"And if you have to come back here to pick him up, anyway, we could have…" She covered her face with her hands, making the rest of her sentence difficult to decipher.

"Sorry, I didn't get that."

She lowered her hands. "If you think it would add to the festive atmosphere for Morgan, we could have cake and balloons waiting here for her. I could also invite over Josh and Natalie."

He was dumbstruck by her generosity. "Not that I'm ungrateful for the offer, but *why?* I got the impression we were already a bit too…underfoot."

"I guess I just really like your kids."

She said it so grudgingly that he knew it was nothing less than the truth. This wasn't an instance of some woman telling him he had cute kids because she wanted to score brownie points with the affluent surgeon. Brenna had seen his children cranky, belligerent, hungry, needy and tired; yet she liked them, anyway.

It really stank that they were being so adult and reasonable about keeping their hands to themselves, because he'd never wanted to kiss her more.

ADAM WAS PROUD of himself for not having to use the "in case of emergency" number Sara had given him. As per her request, the kids had left her a message when they'd reached Mistletoe and checked into the Chattavista, but other than that, they hadn't really spoken to their mother until today. He'd known that she wouldn't miss calling on Morgan's birthday.

The phone rang first thing in the morning as they were all getting ready to go down for breakfast. He would have let Morgan pick it up if she hadn't just started brushing her teeth. Instead, he answered.

"Hello?"

"Adam! It's Sara." She hesitated, as if wanting to ask how things were going but not wanting him to feel interrogated.

"I know three people who are going to be very glad to talk to you," he said, hoping she was enjoying her honeymoon and not worrying about them too much. He passed the phone to Geoff first.

"Hey, Mom! We miss you. But we're having a good time. Like, yesterday, when Morgan had to be rushed to the emergency room and— Oof! Dad has no sense of humor," Geoff complained. "He's throwing things at me… A pillow, but still. Of course I was kidding. Not about the good time, though. We got a cat."

"Hey!" Morgan bounced out of the bathroom, her features scrunched into an expression of indignation. "I want to tell her about that. It's *my* birthday."

"All right, squirt." Geoff ruffled her hair and told his mother goodbye.

Then Morgan was off and running, telling their mother about how they'd adopted a stray cat who would live with Adam in Tennessee, but for now was staying with "Ms. Pierce, the pretty pet-sitter."

That part made Adam flinch a bit.

"Mommy, you won't guess what me and Daddy and Liza are doing today! We're having our toes and fingers painted. They said I could pick any color I want and even pick what music they play in the beauty salon while I'm there."

After that, Eliza took her turn, although she didn't have nearly as much to say as the other two. Her mother must have noticed, because there was a long silence on the Mistletoe end while Sara spoke. Was she giving her daughter a pep talk?

"She wants to speak to you," Eliza said a few minutes later.

Adam put Geoff temporarily in charge and gave the kids permission to go downstairs and start enjoying the breakfast buffet without him. "Keep an eye on Morgan, and I'll be there soon," he told them.

"They're gone?" Sara confirmed. "So. How's it really going?"

He sat on the edge of his bed. "I swear no one's been to the ER. When exactly did Geoff develop such a warped sense of humor, anyway? Sara, I have to tell you, I'm amazed by the job you do. You deal with lost socks and painful crushes and battles of wills every single day, and you're obviously doing something right because they're turning out pretty damn well."

His words of praise were met with shocked silence. "Th-thank you. Guess we all have our skills. I mean, I can sew a Halloween costume with the best of 'em, but you should see my pitiful attempts at coronary-artery-bypass grafting."

He laughed aloud, impressed that she could rattle off the terminology. That probably meant she'd done a better job of listening during their marriage than he had.

"Dan's a lucky man," he told her without rancor.

"Wow. You're just full of pleasant surprises today. Mistletoe must agree with you."

"It's a nice place." Brenna's smile flashed in his mind. "Nice people, too."

"Such as the 'pretty pet-sitter'?" she prodded.

"Brenna Pierce, the woman boarding the cat for us. You'd like her."

"Ah, but the question is, how much do *you* like her?"

"I don't know what you're imagining, but I haven't even been here a full week."

"That is so not an answer," she said, sounding just like Eliza.

He flopped back on the bed. "We probably discussed it at the time, but remind me. How did the kids take it when you and Dan started dating?"

"Pretty well, but I think they were excited to have…" She paused.

"Yes?"

"A father figure in their lives," she concluded apologetically. "I'm thrilled you're taking this vacation with them, I am, and it sounds as if it's going really, really well. But there were birthdays you missed, sporting events you couldn't attend. And they liked having a guy up in the bleachers rooting for them.

"Even then, there was some backsliding," Sara added. "You may have noticed how Eliza can be a tad moody?"

And the *Titanic*'s maiden voyage was a tad choppy. "You don't say."

"The point is, we muddled through. I sat them down and had frank discussions with them about Dan, kept them apprised of where the relationship was going. You and the kids will just have to find your own way. I believe in you." She sounded sincere.

"But just to clarify, *you* don't have a problem with my getting romantically involved with someone?" He had that same involuntary mental image of Brenna again. This time his chest tightened in a not-exactly-painful way.

"Of course not!" Sara said. "As long as you keep the kids' best interests first and foremost, I'd be thrilled for you."

When he got off the phone, he immediately left the room to join the kids. But today, he barely heard the way they ribbed each other or the observations they made about other diners. He was too preoccupied with seeing Brenna later in the day and wrestling with his growing attraction to her. He supposed that, as far as come-on lines went, "Good news! My ex-wife says we can hook up" wasn't very debonair.

"IT MUST HAVE BEEN so cool growing up in your family," Geoff commented from behind the desk.

Surprised by the non sequitur, Brenna studied her office, trying to spot any telltale signs of coolness. "What makes you say that?"

"Well, there's Josh, who's taking us rafting next week." Geoff had explained that Lydia at the lodge would look after Morgan for the afternoon; Brenna had felt inexplicably bereft at this news. Even though she did not have the time to sit with Morgan and lose potentially hours of work, it had occurred to her that the Varners would be gone before she knew it. Would she wish later that she'd had an extra afternoon with the adorably high-spirited girl? "And of course, there's you."

"Of course," Brenna said, grinning.

"So I figured with the way you guys turned out, your family must have been pretty great."

"It was. Is," she admitted. "But it's easier to appreciate those things in retrospect, now that I'm out of the house."

Geoff fidgeted, worrying at his thumbnail. "I probably didn't appreciate my family enough when I had them. You know, before the divorce. I like Dan, my stepdad, but just sometimes I miss…"

She found herself wanting to hug him. "You still have your family, you know. Your mom and dad may not live together, but that doesn't mean they love you any less."

"Yeah, I know. And it doesn't *all* suck. Some days I feel like I see more of Dad now than when he was at home with us. I couldn't believe it when he said he was staying away from the hospital so long just to spend time with us! I think he's having fun. He likes you," Geoff blurted.

"I like him, too." Oh, for crying out loud—was she *blushing?* "So, are you clear on what I need you to do with those?"

Geoff looked in the direction she'd waved, at the motley collection of different-size receipts she'd unearthed from her car, her desk drawers, her purse and half-a-dozen other miscellaneous places. "Yeah, I need to organize all of these by date, and if I finish that, I can cross-reference them into these groups you gave me, like Transportation and Promotion."

"Perfect. Then I'll just—"

"Seriously, I've never seen him like this," Geoff continued smoothly, his train of thought apparently able to run on multiple tracks at a time.

Well, what else should she expect from a generation that grew up with picture-in-picture television and was capable of texting one friend while physically talking with another? *Sheesh.* Nothing like a teenager to make you feel old.

"Do you like him, too?" Geoff asked.

Should she tell him politely but firmly that it was none of his business, or remind him that she'd already said she did?

"Get to work, kid."

He grinned at her. "I'll take that as a yes."

He turned to the task at hand, but she found it difficult to follow suit. What did he mean, he'd never seen his father like this? Maybe Adam was just more relaxed and seemed happier because he was on vacation. *Don't read too much into it.* But she couldn't help feeling secretly pleased.

About fifteen minutes before they expected Adam to show up with the girls, Natalie knocked on Brenna's front door. She had shopping bags hanging on both arms.

"Josh is coming behind me with the cake. It turned out so cute! Let me squeeze in and put this ice cream in your freezer before it starts to melt all over everything."

Brenna's stepbrother approached with a sheet cake balanced across his hands. A large metallic helium balloon with a Puppydale character was tied to his fingers. As Brenna helped them unload the party goodies, she saw that the same adorable, big-eyed puppy was on the napkins and plates.

"She'll love this," Geoff enthused. Then he pulled a face. "Wait, do I have to wear one of these hats?"

The adults assured him that he did, then Natalie showed Brenna the small birthday corsage she'd made at her flower shop for the guest of honor. "Plus, we grabbed these from the Fourth of July display." She held out a couple of boxes of sparklers.

"Cool!" Geoff was definitely more interested in the pyrotechnics than the Puppydale party favors. Cocking his head to the side, he said, "They're here. I just heard Dad's engine cut off."

Brenna tossed him a hat and secured another on her own head. Muttering under his breath, Geoff put it on. Then they all went into the living room and waited quietly.

Adam opened the door for his daughters, and everyone yelled, "Surprise!" when Morgan walked inside. The little girl clapped her hands in delight. Eliza, in contrast, looked leery, as if party hats were immediate cause for suspicion.

While Morgan showed off her pink-and-purple glitter nails to Natalie, the twelve-year-old sidled up to Brenna. "What's the catch?" she demanded.

Brenna sighed. "No catch. There is, however, cake. You like chocolate?"

"Well, duh. Who doesn't?" Eliza frowned. "Are you doing all this because you're crushing on my dad?

Because you said you never date." Her tone rang with accusation.

"I'm doing this because I like Morgan," Brenna said firmly. However much in favor Geoff might be of Brenna and Adam seeing each other romantically, clearly Eliza didn't feel the same way.

"Okay. Good." Eliza turned, but before she walked away, she muttered, "Thank you."

"What she said," Adam echoed, his expression tender. "It was really great of you to go to this trouble."

Her face warmed. "Trouble? You handed me a twenty, Josh and Natalie picked up the cake. It was no big deal."

He pointed to the radiant five-year-old who was adjusting the elastic of a party hat under her chin. "It is to her. Listen, can I talk to you?"

She raised her eyebrows. "As opposed to what we're doing now?"

"Alone."

The single word shivered through her. "Yeah. Hey, guys? Go ahead and put the plates on the table, get candles on that cake. We'll be right back."

She led Adam down the hall, hoping people would assume they were checking on Ellie, and that cake and ice cream would be enough to distract the kids from following.

At the far end of the hallway, she leaned against the wall. "Everything okay?"

He didn't stop coming toward her until his toes

bumped hers. She sucked in a breath as he braced one arm next to her.

"Everything's great. I just wanted to let you know…" He lowered his head, his mouth moving over hers with avid thoroughness.

Her mind went blank. But her body didn't need coherent thought to respond, merely instinct. She rose on her toes, lacing her fingers behind his neck and pulling him even closer. Her lips opened beneath his, and he stroked his tongue inside. His kiss was hungry with need yet unhurried, as if there weren't a roomful of people in the opposite end of the house who might catch them. As if Brenna were the only other person in the world and he'd be content to kiss her for an eternity.

She nearly moaned at the thought, his kiss sending pulses of pleasure throughout her entire body. It had been too long since she'd felt a wanting like this—she wasn't sure it had *ever* been quite like this. So raw and undisciplined. She'd tried to sustain the same control in her love life that she sought in all areas of her life. But now she felt reckless and bold and off balance. It was both exhilarating and terrifying.

Trying to catch her breath, she broke off the kiss, leaning her forehead against the hard plane of his chest. "Well, I hope you're happy. The annual Mistletoe fireworks are going to pale in comparison to *that*."

His low laugh rumbled through her.

She lifted her face. "Don't take this as a complaint, but I thought we weren't going to—?"

"I'd thought not acting on the way I feel about you would be best for the kids."

The way he *felt?* Did he mean the palpable attraction between them—or more? Her heart thudded wildly, but she found she didn't quite have the confidence to ask for clarification. Did it really matter? Either way, he'd be gone within the next two weeks. She was curious to hear the rest of his explanation, though.

"This morning, I talked to someone who changed my mind," he said simply.

"Geoff?" That might explain the boy's earlier conversational gambits.

"No, why would you think that? It's not like I get my romantic advice from a fifteen-year-old." He was a smidge defensive, amusingly so.

"It seemed likely since Geoff was trying to give *me* romantic advice. He didn't come right out and say that you and I should get together, but he hinted at it. Strongly."

Adam grinned. "Smart boy, my son."

"Hey! Aren't you guys coming back?" Morgan called. Her voice escalated as she asked, signaling that she was headed for them.

Adam sprang away, putting a respectable distance between himself and Brenna. "Be right there, sweetie." Then he dropped his voice. "Can we talk about this more?"

"'Talk'?" She waggled her eyebrows.

"Well." He shot her one last sizzling glance that his daughter couldn't see from behind him. "Among other things."

Chapter Eleven

Even though the local bakery was known for its delectable creations, Brenna could barely taste the chocolate cake. Her senses were too focused on Adam. She tried not to stare or show any physical awareness inappropriate to a five-year-old's birthday party, but she questioned whether she was doing a sufficient job of hiding her interest, because Josh was openly smirking at her behind Adam's back.

Morgan had apparently made her peace with Ellie being her birthday present, plus she'd already opened gifts from her mother and stepfather, so she wasn't expecting anything else. She squealed with joy when Brenna produced a gift bag.

"Don't get too excited," Brenna preempted her. "It's just a couple of little things I picked up for you and threw in. I don't want you thinking there's a pony in there."

Morgan eyeballed the small bag and laughed. "Josh, your sister is funny."

"Tell me about it."

The birthday girl fished out a pink collar Brenna had picked up for Ellie and an easy-to-read guide on cat care that was also a coloring book. "Thank you, Brenna!" She hopped down from her chair to snag a hug.

Brenna squatted down to return the embrace, surprised by the sense of sweetness that overcame her. *I could get used to this.* When she glanced up, Adam was watching her so intently her skin burned.

"Since it's not as much fun to do the sparklers until it gets darker," Josh said, "I thought we could play a birthday game first."

As he pulled a thin felt mat out of a bag, it occurred to Brenna for the first time what a good father he was going to make. The thought cheered her. She'd never quite been able to imagine herself as a mom—for years, her self-defense mechanism had been to think immediately of something else any time her mind veered toward mothers—but she found that she loved the idea of being an aunt.

Until this month she'd always known she was "an animal person" but had never suspected she might be "a kid person." Children were too reliant on others, too fragile. She'd worry about letting one down; she'd fear looking into their small, trusting faces and seeing the vulnerable girl she'd once been.

Josh's game turned out to be a modernized take on the classic pin-the-tail-on-the-donkey. Only in this version, where Velcro was used instead of sharp implements, the blindfolded player was trying to successfully place a soft white bone in the puppy's waiting mouth.

Behind her, Adam said sotto voce, "No animals were harmed in the making of this game," and Brenna giggled.

Later, as they all stood in Brenna's front yard with sparklers, her stepbrother confronted her in a whisper. "Admit it, Natalie and I were right. See how much fun a double date can be?"

She glanced to where Adam stood with Morgan, and her heart contracted. *Fun* was too frivolous a word for the pull of poignant, unpredictable emotions inside her.

Trying to keep her voice lighter than she felt, she protested, "I'm admittedly out of practice, but I'm not sure you can call this a date. Too much scrutiny. I couldn't even hold his hand without worrying about how it would affect three minors."

"I see what you mean." He pursed his lips thoughtfully. "You know, Natalie and I were just talking about that new animated movie coming out and how we'd feel silly going to see it without taking any kids with us. Think Adam would let us borrow his one night this week?"

All the longing she'd been trying to suppress since Adam kissed her bubbled to the surface at the thought of stealing some private time with him. They'd never been truly alone. "You are the best brother in the world."

He slung an arm over her shoulders. "I've been telling you that for years."

ADAM PARKED the car in the visitors' lot at Kerrigan Farms, glancing appreciatively at the endless stretch of vast blue sky. "Can't ask for a prettier Sunday afternoon than this, can you?"

"Nope," Morgan agreed cheerfully.

"I don't think he actually needed an answer," Eliza said, oozing condescension. "It's called a rhetorical question."

Adam spun around to fix his middle child with a paternal glare. "She can answer if she wants. What's got you in such a bad mood?"

Her only response was to glare back at him.

He was truly baffled. Everyone had seemed to have fun at Brenna's Friday evening, and yesterday they had an innocuous combination of hiking to a nearby waterfall, shooting pool at the lodge and going to the actual pool. Where, Adam had been relieved to notice, Bobby the Punk Lifeguard had been replaced for the day by a patrician-featured woman in her mid-twenties. It had been a relaxed, enjoyable day, despite all the times he'd found himself thinking of Brenna and their upcoming date Tuesday night. He'd practically hugged Josh in gratitude when the guy had asked if he and Natalie could take the kids out for pizza and a movie.

It was irrational how *much* Adam looked forward to seeing her again. Could he possibly be missing a woman he'd seen only a day and a half ago? There was a slim possibility their paths would cross this evening. She'd agreed that he and the kids could stop by on their way back from the farm to visit Ellie for a few minutes, but Brenna wasn't sure she'd be home from her appointments.

"You know where the key is," she'd said. "Feel free to let yourself in."

He'd thanked her, hoping he sounded gracious and completely unlike a man needy for her company. If she *was* home, the most he could hope for was casual conversation benign enough for young ears and, if he was lucky, a quick, hard kiss goodbye such as the one he'd stolen Friday on the pretext of having left his wallet in her house.

Seeing his own grin in the rearview mirror, Adam reflected that it was ridiculous how much the prospect of small talk and a pilfered kiss cheered him.

The four of them got out of the SUV and strolled down a shaded path to the welcome booth, where he paid the nominal entrance fee.

The woman there introduced herself as Kasey Kerrigan and handed them a map of the farm. "See these *X*'s? Those indicate where Ben's set up coolers. They're stocked with ice and bottles of water. Please, help yourself. The last thing we want is someone passing out because of sunstroke or dehydration. We do have a doctor visiting this afternoon, but I'm sure he'd rather enjoy his day off than administer emergency first aid," she said with a smile.

"My daddy's a doctor, too!" Morgan informed her.

"Oh? Varner…" Kasey repeated his last name as if

trying to recall whether she'd heard it before. "Are you one of the new docs they've hired at the medical complex?"

"No, ma'am. Just here for a few weeks to enjoy Mistletoe with my kids."

"Well, have fun!"

Adam handed the map to Geoff so the three kids could consult it together. "What do we want to do first?"

Morgan didn't even have to think about it. "Petting zoo!"

Eliza snorted. "Petting zoos are for babies."

"Are not! Dad—"

"Eliza, apologize to your sister."

She did so. Resentfully.

"Maybe I can't mandate a good mood the way I can a curfew, but I *can* tell you to stop inflicting your annoyance on everyone else. Understood?" When she nodded, Adam gentled his tone. "Do you want to talk about what's wrong?"

"I just don't feel good," she mumbled. "Let's go check out those animals now. Might as well get this over with."

Adam sighed. "That's the spirit."

ADAM STOOD IN LINE behind an older man at a make-shift concession stand. The Varners had downed several bottles of water so far, but now Morgan was saying she could use food. *And I could use a stiff drink.* Today had not been an overwhelming hit. Though Morgan was having fun, Geoff didn't seem to think that picking his own blueberries ranked up there with white-water rafting or even playing video games on his DS back at the Chattavista. Then there was Eliza.

The animals had been "smelly," she claimed to be "dying of the heat," and when he'd handed her a cold water to help cool off, she'd complained that it tasted funny.

Now the three children sat on a nearby bench while Adam waited to buy snacks and soft drinks. Since Morgan and Eliza had been at each other's throats for the past couple of hours, he was relieved when a little boy about Morgan's age wandered over to her and engaged her in a conversation about a cartoon she and Geoff sometimes watched together. She'd tried to explain some of the creatures and their origins to Adam, but he mostly remained clueless.

Now Morgan chatted happily as Adam paid the vendor. Eliza could either sulk in silence or pick a fight with her brother, but he figured Geoff could handle himself. When Adam turned, he saw that the man who'd been in front of him in line was now standing with the little boy.

The man, round but not overweight with a head of thick gray hair, nodded a greeting to Adam. "Seems like my grandson and your little girl have some common interests."

Adam distributed drinks and soft jumbo pretzels while the two five-year-olds talked some more. Upon learning that Morgan was the same age as him, the boy got excited about the possibility of Morgan being in his kindergarten class.

"Nah, we live too far away," Morgan said. "We're visiting from Tennessee."

"First time in Mistletoe?" the boy's grandfather asked Morgan, "or do you have family in the area?"

"First time," she said.

"Welcome to our town. I hope you're enjoying your stay. I'm Gerald Kimborough and this is my grandson, Todd."

Adam whipped his head around. "Dr. Gerald Kimborough, the nephrologist?"

The other man laughed. "You must either be in the medical profession yourself or you know a patient of mine."

"Dr. Adam Varner." He held out a hand. "Cardio. I like to stay current on other disciplines. I read that case study you had published on renal-transplantation patients. But I thought it mentioned that you were a nephrology fellow up in New England."

"I was. My wife's family is from Georgia, though, and our daughter settled here. I moved down to help run the new dialysis facility. Mistletoe has an active retirement community, along with a great seniors center and newly expanding medical complex. We're building such a great reputation that some patients north of Atlanta are choosing to make the drive up here to see us, instead of going into the metro area for treatment.

Drawing more doctors, too, for kidney treatment and the cardio unit.

"It's a chance to keep doing what I do best, but in a different environment from where I was before. Plus," he added with a fond smile at the towheaded child, "now I get to spend more time with the big guy."

"Dad!" Eliza's tone was so impatient that she'd obviously been waiting for a break in the conversation. "We've fed goats, we've picked berries. Can we *go* now?"

Anger surged through Adam that she could continue to be so ungrateful after he'd tried for days on end to spend time with them and help them have fun. He turned to her. "I know it's hot outside, but you're sitting in the shade and you have a cold drink. Cutting short other people's fun because you're bored is just selfish," he admonished. "You had a manicure the day before yesterday, got to explore a waterfall, are going rafting tomorrow and are planning to see a movie on Tuesday, to say nothing of the big Fourth of July celebration. Not every second can be go, go, go, Eliza. You're twelve, which is mature enough to stop acting like a spoiled brat!"

She recoiled as if he'd slapped her, her expression stricken. When tears welled up in her eyes, she mumbled an "Excuse me" and bolted for the nearby restroom. Watching her hasty exit, Adam felt like an ogre.

Dr. Kimborough cleared his throat, looking embarrassed. "Yes, well, lovely to have met you. Todd, let's run along so the Varners can finish up their tour of the farm."

"I'm sorry," Adam said. "I—"

The doctor waved his hand. "Not at all. I had a teenage daughter once myself. Gets easier after their twenty-first birthday," he whispered conspiratorially.

How lovely, Adam thought. Now he had something to look forward to—nine more years of hell. Of course, in nine years, *Morgan* would be a teenager. He groaned.

Once the Kimboroughs had departed, Geoff stood. "Way to go, Dad."

Adam squeezed his eyes shut. "Son, I could do without the sarcasm right now."

"No, I was being sincere. Way to go, congratulations. You normally tiptoe around Eliza, letting her act however she wants. Mom would never have put up with that."

"Oh." He processed this. "Good to know. I guess."

He'd never meant to give the impression that Eliza could do whatever she wanted without consequences. Although to be fair, most of her transgressions were of the mere eye-rolling kind; it wasn't as if she'd been sneaking cigarettes outside the lodge or boosting cars on Main Street.

It was strangely bolstering that Geoff thought he was acting like a real parent now. On par with Sara. Did that mean Adam was making progress, even though one of his children was currently not speaking to him? Some parts of this parenting gig were less fun than others.

When five minutes had passed, Geoff glanced at Eliza's untouched pretzel. "Can I have it?"

Adam answered with a quelling look. Another few minutes ticked by. "Morgan, pumpkin, would you mind going into the restroom and asking your sister if she could please join the rest of us?"

"She's gonna yell at me," Morgan predicted.

"If she does, I promise I will deal with that."

Morgan disappeared into the women's room, and a moment later returned with a subdued and tearstained older sister.

"Daddy?" Morgan ventured. "It's okay with me if we leave now. I wanna see Ellie, anyway."

Accepting defeat, he carried Morgan's plastic bucket of blueberries so that she could have both hands for her drink while they walked toward the exit.

"We should give some of these berries to Brenna," Geoff said. When Adam had noted earlier that Geoff had stopped calling her Ms. Pierce, his son had joked that it was because they were "practically co-workers" now: "I helped her prepare for taxes next quarter. Check me, I'm like an accountant."

"That's a nice idea," Adam said. "And don't forget, Lydia at the lodge said that if you bring her enough berries, she'll make sure you guys get blueberry pancakes for breakfast tomorrow."

Halfway to Brenna's house, Adam realized Eliza hadn't said a word the entire time. His first assumption was that she was giving him the silent treatment, but when he noticed the way she'd cradled her arms against her abdomen, his conscience plagued him. She *had* complained she wasn't feeling well, but it had been a nonspecific gripe on the heels of him asking about her ornery mood, so he hadn't lent it much credence.

As they drove down Brenna's street, Morgan remarked, "No car in the driveway."

Adam had already noticed this and was doing his level best not to broadcast his disappointment. *You'll see her Tuesday.* That was only two nights from now.

He parked in the driveway and everyone hopped out. Zoe met them at the fence, wagging her tail so hard her body shook. They went inside, and Adam tried not to notice the sheer Brenna-ness of the place. The faint, lingering scent of her body lotion, a book she'd been reading left facedown on an end table. He stole a peek at the title and smiled—he enjoyed that particular series, too. Considering the slightly dusty book jacket, she'd probably started this one before her summer schedule ramped up into high gear.

Morgan ran down the hall, already talking to Ellie in that slightly higher-than-normal voice she used with animals. He resolved that he was giving the kids ten minutes, fifteen tops, before they left for Chattavista. There would be no dawdling in the hopes of catching Brenna as she came through the door.

Geoff disappeared into Brenna's office; he hadn't quite finished the odd jobs she'd given him the other day, and she'd told him that she'd pay him for any time he put in, whether she was here or not. Whenever he talked about doing one of the errands she'd assigned, he swelled with pride. Adam made a mental note to revisit the employment issue with Sara. He understood why she'd initially told Geoff that he couldn't have a job on top of school, but if Geoff could keep his grades up, maybe it was time to change that.

It dawned on Adam that, in the past couple of years, he'd been far too passive. He'd felt guilty over not being there, so he defaulted to Sara's opinion on everything as if he didn't have a right to disagree with her. Though he wouldn't undermine her by arguing a point in front of the kids, it was time he gave more thought to their lives and offered real input, not just financial support.

Since the television remote was on the coffee table, he flipped on the TV and went to one of those all-news channels. He wasn't sure when exactly Eliza ducked out of the kitty den, but a bit later, Geoff and Morgan both appeared in front of him.

"I finished everything Brenna laid out for me," Geoff said with satisfaction.

"I'm still playing with Ellie, but you said fifteen minutes," Morgan reminded him. "It's been fifteen."

Already? In spite of himself, Adam's gaze went to the window and the driveway beyond. "Where's your sister?"

Geoff gave an exaggerated shrug, accompanied by a "women" eye roll. "Bathroom. Again."

"Something's wrong with her," Morgan declared, her gamine face puckered with worry.

Adam was starting to agree. "Why don't you guys go out in the yard and play with Zoe? I'll take care of Eliza."

After they'd done as suggested, he knocked lightly on the bathroom door. Unless he was mistaken, there was sniffling coming inside. "Eliza, honey? Are you okay?"

"No!" More pronounced sniffling. Then she muttered something too low to hear followed by an emphatic, "I want Mom!"

"I know you and your mother are a lot closer than you and I have been lately, but I want to change that." He sat on the floor, feeling a bit stupid for baring his soul to a doorknob. "You can talk to me about anything, I promise."

"Not about *this!*" She sounded horrified, and her voice cracked. He felt powerless with his little girl crying on the other side of a locked door. "Could you please *just get Mom on the phone?*"

Then it clicked. The likely reason she'd been so cranky and on the verge of tears, the way she'd been holding her stomach as if in pain. "Oh, honey. Are you—?"

"I don't want to talk to you about it! I'd die of humiliation."

Forget that he was specially trained in the workings of the human body; for this, a girl needed her mother. "Be right back!"

He returned to the living room and dialed Sara's cell number, although it took him several tries to get it right. Why were his hands shaking? This was a natural biological process that all females went through. *Yes, but she's only...twelve.*

How had twelve years passed already? He vividly remembered the day she was born, so much tinier than Geoff had been, how she'd seemed so fragile in Adam's hands that he'd been scared he might hurt her. Then she'd screwed up her reddened face, opened her mouth and let loose with a yowl that had made the nurse and an exhausted Sara cringe but Adam laugh. He'd known then that something that could make such a ferocious noise wasn't as frail as she looked.

Over the phone, his ex-wife's recorded voice instructed him to leave a message.

"Sara? Oh, Sara, I wish you'd picked up! Look, it's not an emergency per se—kids are fine—but call as soon as you get this, okay? Anytime day or night! *Any*time."

It wasn't until he disconnected that he realized he was panicking. He could have just told Sara what the issue was, but he was having trouble wrapping his mind around it. Preoccupied with the situation and what he should say to Eliza, he missed both the car outside and the steps on the porch. He jumped in surprise when the front door swung open and Brenna entered the living room.

"Oh, thank God, a *woman!*" He darted forward and took hold of her hand.

Her eyebrows shot up. "Well, you get points for enthusiasm. Although you might want to practice being more discerning than that."

"We're having a crisis." He dropped her hand, abashed. What had he been planning to do, drag her bodily down the hall and dump everything in her lap? "A, erm, *female* crisis." He sounded more like a socially awkward seventh grader than a medical professional.

He tried again. "Apparently Eliza is…she's started—"

"Oh!" Brenna clucked her tongue. "Poor baby. You want me to go talk to her?"

"Please." He felt almost light-headed with relief.

Sitting on the couch, he listened as Brenna approached the closed door. *Please don't push her away,* he silently advised Eliza. He knew she'd rather have Sara right now, understandably so, but he hoped that his daughter wouldn't distance herself from others at her own expense.

After a moment, the door opened, and he heard the soft background murmur of female voices. And a few seconds later, Brenna returned, palming her keys.

"Eliza and I are going for a little shopping excursion. I can take her back to the lodge when we're finished. Why don't we just meet you there?"

"I can't thank you enough."

She flashed him a cheeky smile. "You can try. Tuesday night."

Chapter Twelve

"Thank you," Eliza mumbled as they left the drugstore. "That was embarrassing, but it would have been worse with my dad."

"You're welcome. I realize that kids—young women," she amended, unlocking the car doors, "probably hate it when adults say this, but I know how you feel. My mom wasn't around for my first period, either."

It had been mortifying. Even though Brenna had taken the same health classes as her peers and had, in theory, known what to expect, her first thought had been *I'm bleeding to death!* It had hurt.

"Where was your mom?"

"Don't know," Brenna confided. "Still don't. She brought me to Mistletoe and married Fred just a few months later—Fred is Josh's dad. Then she took off for the store and none of us ever saw her again, although Fred did find a note afterward."

Eliza's jaw dropped, her own misery temporarily forgotten. "She just *left?* And she didn't even tell you goodbye? That's way worse than being twenty minutes late for the sixth-grade graduation ceremony or being a no-show at the father-daughter volleyball picnic."

Brenna knew that if Adam had missed an event for one of his kids, it had to have been something critical that kept him. He'd probably been off nobly saving a life, people around him yelling *Clear!* or *Clamp!* or *Stat!* the way they always did in medical dramas. But still, she empathized with the sense of loss the girl must have felt.

"Now that I'm older, I realize that even though her leaving hurt badly for a long time, it might have been for the best." By the time they'd reached Mistletoe, Brenna had already become tense and brittle, afraid to form attachments. Who knew when they'd pick up and go again? How long a current boyfriend would last? When her mercurial mother might turn on her? "In fact, her disappearing like that might even have been her way of protecting me. Maybe she did it because she loved me."

"Pfftt." Eliza snorted. "Whatever. It still sucks."

Brenna laughed. "Yeah. It still sucks." She turned her key in the ignition, relieved when the car started. For what she'd paid to mortgage it out of the garage, the vehicle should be so finely tuned it could qualify for the Indy 500.

"You hungry?" Brenna asked. "We can swing by a drive-through somewhere."

"Nah."

"Forget dinner, then. What about just a chocolate

milk shake? Great cure for cramps," Brenna added. A decent milk shake helped keep *her* from killing anyone at the wrong time of the month.

Eliza perked up a bit. "Yeah, okay. Sounds good."

They were nearly to the lodge and happily slurping down shakes when Eliza resurrected the topic of Brenna's mom. "You're really not mad at her?"

"Why should I be? Letting anger fester hurts me more than it hurts her, wherever she is."

"I guess. Did you know she was going to leave? Was it out of the blue, or did she sort of slowly slip out of your life before going for good?"

Brenna's gaze flitted to her young passenger. "How do you mean?"

"Like ignoring you. Not calling when she was supposed to. Guess that didn't matter, since you lived with her." Eliza's gaze slid to the hands clasped tightly in her lap. "My mom got a divorce because Dad wasn't really paying attention to anything but work. You'd think he would have apologized, sent flowers."

Maybe, but relationships were complicated and there had probably been other factors at play. Brenna kept the thought to herself, not wanting to discourage Eliza from safely venting.

"But it didn't help much. Even if he showed up, half the time he'd get an emergency page." Her eyes glistened with tears. "Does it make me selfish that sometimes I didn't care who he was off saving, that I just wanted him to be with me?"

"I don't think so. You're completely entitled to want your dad's love, and his time. But, honey, your father is nothing like my mom. She was…unwell. He isn't going anywhere. He's crazy about you three. Don't you think this trip is proof of that?"

Eliza eyed her skeptically, then shrugged. "He's been my dad for nearly thirteen years. This trip is twenty days."

BY THE TIME they reached the lodge, Eliza was barely smothering her yawns. She shuffled toward the Varners' suite with the appearance of someone who was sleepwalking. Adam must have been listening for them, because he opened the door just as Brenna started to knock.

Brenna handed the girl the bag of feminine supplies they'd purchased, including some neon-bright fingernail polish and a fashion magazine for young women.

"Thank you," Eliza said. "And, Dad? Sorry I was a pita today."

His eyebrows drew together. "Pita?"

"You know, PITA? Pain in the… Anyway, I'll try to do better."

He kissed her on the forehead. "Go rest up for our white-water rafting adventure tomorrow afternoon. That is, if you think you're up to it?"

"Wouldn't miss it!" Despite her fatigue, the genuine anticipation in her voice was unmistakable.

"Well, just let me know if you change your mind. I'm flexible."

With Eliza preparing for bed and Morgan and Geoff engrossed in a rented movie, Adam was free to walk Brenna back downstairs. He seemed in no hurry to get rid of her, though.

Nodding toward the two-person swing on the veranda, he said, "Sit with me for a few minutes? Or do you need to rush back out and do more pet visits?"

"I have four more tonight, but they can wait another twenty minutes." She'd gotten up so early that morning, before the sun, that when she'd returned home this afternoon, it had been with optimistic plans of catching a catnap. Now she didn't have time for that.

Besides, being alone with Adam rejuvenated her. She experienced something like adrenaline, but warmer and less jittery. She was alert, her senses heightened by his nearness.

The swing jostled under their combined weight, and Brenna let herself sway toward him. Until meeting Adam, she hadn't realized how deficient of touch her life had become. Her animals considered a pat on the head or a belly rub a crucial part of the day, but except for occasionally shaking hands with a new client or maybe hugging someone at Sunday family dinners, it had been too long since Brenna had been this close to another human.

"Thank you," he murmured. "I don't know what we would have done today if you hadn't come along."

"Oh, you would have muddled through. It would have been awkward, possibly hostile on her part, and you would have made a silent pact never to speak of it again…but you would have handled it."

"Is she okay?" he asked.

Brenna nodded. "I helped her select some over-the-counter pain medicine. She said she didn't have any weird allergies that she knew of and wasn't currently taking anything. I gave her a crash course on her best options if she wants to go rafting tomorrow. I also…talked to her some in the car. Not just about this."

He straightened, looking not only curious but nearly reverent, as if Brenna were about to hand him the Holy Grail of Understanding Your Adolescent Daughter. "Yeah?"

"She's ticked off at you," Brenna said bluntly. "But more than that, she's scared you won't be around for her."

He clenched a fist against his thigh. "I suppose I deserve that. Sara and I were practically kids ourselves, newly married when we got pregnant with Geoff. She did such a beautiful job handling motherhood while I finished up med school. I don't mean to make excuses, but the hours for an intern are hellish. Once you make resident, they upgrade you to merely purgatorial."

"Adam. You don't owe me any explanations."

"I know. I just… Do you mind my telling you about this?"

"No, I like hearing about you. Even the imperfect parts," she assured him.

"I specialize in those," he drawled, looking angry

with himself. "I didn't mean to take Sara for granted or dump everything on her. I think it truly didn't dawn on me that she needed help. She had the kids organized and scheduled, knew just where she wanted everything and who liked what favorite bear or blanket. When things got bad enough that she complained, I really did try to pitch in. And I ended up feeling as if I were just in the way, like an intruder in my own family."

Brenna had some experience with feeling like the outsider, a jarring angle in the family circle.

"I know I've screwed up," he said. "But I didn't realize I'd screwed up so badly that my own daughter is afraid I won't be there."

"Well—" she caught her bottom lip between her teeth "—I may not have helped. I was trying to relate, told her a bit about my own childhood."

Adam tilted back to better see her expression. "Problems with your dad?"

"My mom." Her voice was barely audible. *I never talk about this.* For good reason. People threw around words like *healing* and *closure*. Closure? That was a laugh—the woman was God knows where on the globe. Assuming she was even still alive and well.

Brenna swallowed hard. "My mom brought me to Mistletoe when I was around Eliza's age. She met Fred Pierce, Josh's father. His own divorce hadn't been final all that long, and I think they rebounded into each other."

"Had your parents been divorced long?" Adam asked quietly.

"I never knew my dad. She left him when she was pregnant with me." Leaving people, her great legacy. "I think…I don't know, but I think she was sick. For months she'd seem okay. There would even be days where she was better than okay. Waking me up in the middle of the night and asking me if I wanted to go on an 'adventure' with her. One time when we lived in Kentucky, it was to go out in the first snowfall of the season. We found a twenty-four-hour store and bought chocolate bars. It was midnight, and I was gorging on chocolate and having a snowball fight with my mom."

Brenna stopped, her throat tight. For some reason, it hurt more to remember candy bars in the snow—had she ever told anyone about that?—than it did to recall being abandoned.

"At times like that, I thought she was the best mother in the world. I was *awed* by her. But then there were her short-tempered moments. A lot less fun," she said sardonically. "And long periods of time where she was quiet. I don't remember seeing her cry, but she was just so damn palpably unhappy. I used to wonder if it was somehow my fault. Then she'd announce she was getting a new job or that we were going to move to a new apartment, instead of renewing our lease. The change of scenery usually helped. When Fred met her, she was having one of her better times. She seemed stable for a while." Brenna had dared to hope that Mistletoe was some kind of magic place. It had certainly seemed that way through a child's eyes.

"I'm guessing that stability didn't last?" Adam's voice was comforting. Deep, compassionate, but not thick with the oppressive pity she'd feared.

She shook her head. "I could tell it was going to fall apart. She started getting restless, irritable. I was trying to get her attention one day to find out if I could go to a slumber party, and it was like I couldn't get through to her. So I just kept saying 'Mom,' repeatedly, louder and louder. She slapped me. I don't think she meant to."

He squeezed her shoulder. "I'm sorry, Brenna."

"Neither of us told Fred about that. She was gone a week later, and I...I really liked Mistletoe. I loved having a little brother and not being an only child. And maybe because he was already a father, I bonded with Fred a lot faster than I did with the other men who'd been in her life. When I thought the cycle was starting all over again, I was terrified I'd have to give them up. But I didn't. She just took off for parts unknown. Without me."

The memories with her mother in them were crystal clear to this day, but the memory of Fred handing her the note, so Brenna could see for herself that her mom had no intention of coming back—*that she didn't want me*—was hazy. Like something warped and half-remembered from a bad dream.

"By the time Fred could legally divorce her, his first wife was sick and they were already headed down the path to reconciliation. I had something new to be terrified about. At least my mother's 'Dr. Jekyll, Mrs.

Hyde' cycle was a known quantity. But Maggie? I guess I'd read too many fairy tales with evil stepmothers, because the entire time she and Fred were dating, I expected her to insist it was either her or me. But Maggie's wonderful."

"I should expect so. For you to turn out the way you did in spite of everything speaks to their being loving parents—and your being an extraordinarily strong woman." Adam gave her an assessing look as if seeing her for the first time. Or as if he was glimpsing something he'd overlooked before.

Brenna squirmed under the penetrating scrutiny. But she relaxed slightly as he began trailing his hand up and down her back. Lord, his touch felt good.

"Most people," he concluded, "having gone through that kind of emotional turmoil, wouldn't become as bighearted as you are, so generous and giving."

Brenna snorted, then checked herself. *Been spending too much time with Eliza.* "You haven't known me that long. Kevin and I split up because I was too aloof and inaccessible."

"Inaccessible? You? Did he suffer some kind of trauma to the head?" Adam's confusion seemed authentic rather than feigned on her behalf.

She chuckled, snuggling closer. "You're good for my self-esteem."

"Brenna, you're a beautiful woman with the smarts and discipline to start her own successful company, you're good with animals and children, and you kiss like no one's business. Why would your self-esteem need my help?"

She thought about telling him that he saw her differently from others because, with him, she *was* different. Maybe it was easier to be herself with Adam because she'd always known he was leaving. Since there was no chance of him becoming a long-term fixture in her life, there was minimal risk. Or was it more than that? He evoked reactions from her other men didn't.

She didn't know why. Nor did she care to analyze it further, her psyche having been sufficiently probed for one night. "You've been a great listener, and I'm looking forward to seeing you Tuesday night, but I should be going."

"One kiss goodbye?" he asked.

In answer, she pressed closer to him. He tilted her chin up with his finger and captured her mouth.

White heat flashed in her blood, purging unpleasant memories and emotional uncertainties, leaving only sensation. She gripped the front of his shirt with both hands and held on for the ride, kissing him back urgently, coasting on a rising swell of desire. Adam leaned into her as if he couldn't get close enough, and somehow she found herself in a nearly horizontal position, the swing rocking hectically beneath them.

She felt as if she were drowning in the most pleasurable way, breathing in only Adam, letting him blot out all else. Submerged in bliss and craving more, she slid his hand to her breast and arched into his palm.

If they'd kept going at that frenzied pace, she might have ended up making love to him right there on the front porch of the Chattavista Lodge.

Instead, they both sprang apart when, around the corner, the door to the main entrance opened and shut. Breathing hard, they stared at each other, wide-eyed in the shadows. Brenna remembered how Quinn had spoken of "sparks," but this hadn't been some tiny ember alighting randomly where it might become more or might just as easily be snuffed out. This had been a tidal wave of pent-up need that she'd never even noticed until she was in Adam's arms.

"That was your idea of a goodbye?" she asked incredulously. Because it had felt much more like *hello,* the start of something cataclysmic and inevitable.

"If I was doing it wrong," he said with studied innocence, "I'd be happy to practice until I get it right."

"Wow, you doctors really are perfectionists." Her blithe tone was an act, because inside she was reeling.

If being with Adam got any *more* perfect, how would she merrily bid him farewell in a week?

Chapter Thirteen

Adam waited until Tuesday morning at breakfast to have The Talk with his kids. "Hey, guys, there's something I want to discuss with you."

Geoff nodded, not even lowering his fork, and both girls looked up from their plates in silent expectation.

"At the beginning of our trip, I said I wasn't ready to date anyone. That…may have changed."

"Dating like Mommy and Daddy Dan did?" Morgan asked.

"Yes," he said slowly, "but just because they got married doesn't mean I will. Especially not anytime soon."

Morgan sniffed. "*I* think you should marry Brenna."

Eliza gasped. "He's only known her for two weeks! And Brenna isn't interested in him."

"What?" Adam couldn't stop the question from escaping.

"She told me," Eliza said matter-of-factly. "We were talking about how she didn't think dating was worth all the trouble and—"

"You're so full of it," her brother accused. "Brenna told *me* that she does like him!"

Adam whirled around to face his son. "You were discussing this with her, too?"

"No need to thank me, Dad. Just being your wing-man."

Adam's mouth opened, then closed again. No sound emerged. Wearily, he looked at Morgan. "By any chance, did you also have a chat with Brenna about whether or not she should date me?"

"Nope. We mostly talk about Ellie the cat."

"Okay." He took a deep breath, determined to get the conversation back on track. "I'm not marrying anyone. Not now, possibly not ever, we'll just have to see. But I would like to go out with Brenna tonight." Although technically they'd planned to stay in.

"No!" Eliza looked outraged.

"Excuse me?"

"I don't think you should date her."

"After everything she's done for you and your brother and sister?" Adam was startled by how force-fully she objected to the idea. "What can you possibly have against her?"

"But you said you weren't going to."

"I know. And I'm sorry for any confusion. I've changed my mind, though. I want you to know I didn't do it lightly," he told her. "I talked to your mama, too. And Brenna herself. And now I want to talk it over with you kids, keep you fully involved in what's going on in my life."

"Are you in love with her?" Eliza challenged.

The obvious answer was no, but somehow he got distracted giving it. He was too busy remembering the first time he'd seen Brenna, there on the side of the road. The sound of her wry, husky laugh. The party she'd thrown for Morgan. The way she kissed.

"Eliza, men and women don't *start* dating because they're in love. They date to find out if they're compatible, to see if, under the right circumstances, they could love each other. None of this changes how much I love you guys, though."

Morgan tried to ask, "What 'right circumstances'?"

But Eliza overrode her with, "A week from now you'll be back at that *hospital*." She spat the word at him like an obscenity. "Even if you think you're 'compatible,' what's the point?"

His mind skittered to the kisses he'd shared with Brenna on the porch swing. They had unfinished business, but that was hardly an appropriate answer.

"I'm not sure yet," he admitted. "Some things you just don't know until after the fact. But I've known almost since I met her that Brenna Pierce is a special person. Does anyone disagree with that?"

A moment passed, and no one said anything. *She's won us all over.* Miracle of miracles, the four of them agreed on something.

"Then it's settled," he declared. "I'm seeing her tonight."

JOSH HAD DONE a great job as a rafting guide—keeping them safe and informed, but entertained, too—and the kids were thrilled to see him Tuesday evening.

"Everyone got their shoes on?" he asked as he stepped into the suite. "Nat's waiting down in the car."

"Almost ready," Morgan called from the girls' shared bedroom. "Eliza's helping me fix my hair."

Adam faced Geoff. "Why don't you grab my wallet off the nightstand? I want to make sure you guys have plenty of money for the food and the movie tickets."

When it was just the two men, Josh said cheerfully, "Give Brenna a hug for me, and you two have fun tonight. Just…be careful. This is kind of my fault."

Adam blinked. "I don't follow."

Josh glanced away, his expression almost guilty. "I've been nagging her for a couple of months to go out with somebody, anybody. And now here you are."

Somebody, anybody? Adam's lips twitched.

"That sounded bad," Josh said, backpedaling. "All I meant was, Bren can be a really private person. She doesn't open up to others easily."

Thinking of the other night on the lodge porch, Adam raised his eyebrows. Was it possible that her stepbrother didn't know her as well as he thought? Sure, she hadn't introduced herself on that first day with "Hi, I'm Brenna, my mother abandoned me and I have trust issues," which would have been freaky, but in only a couple of weeks, she'd taken Adam into her confidence. She was funny and compassionate, honest and good-natured with his kids. She'd not only had them in her home several times, she'd given them permission to be there even when she wasn't. Hardly a closed-off misanthrope.

"I've been encouraging her to take chances," Josh recapped. "And now she is! So I'm going to feel like crap if you end up hurting her."

"Not half as crappy as I'd feel," Adam said, a little offended that Josh thought he needed to issue a protective warning. "Trust me, I really like your sister."

Massive understatement.

The last time Adam had cared for a woman this much, he'd gone on to marry her.

DARN QUINN for having a life anyway.

Brenna had called the woman in hopes of her coming over for wardrobe consultation, but Quinn was away on a long weekend with friends at a beach house and wouldn't be back until tomorrow. Brenna improvised by modeling different outfits—deliberately feminine and sexy versus not-trying-too-hard, "nonchalantly sexy"—for the dog and cats. For the most part, the animals seemed undecided, viewing all clothes merely as objects on which to shed.

Finally Brenna chose a deep-blue sundress with a flirty knee-length skirt and shoulder straps that tied into simple knots over her bare arms. She doublechecked to make sure no strand of cat or dog hair had made it onto the fabric. Not wanting to be overdressed for an evening at home, she left off shoes and jewelry. The look was simple and pretty.

Too antsy to just sit and wait for Adam's arrival, she shooed the animals out into the yard and sunporch, then checked on dinner. She'd put in a lasagna earlier, setting the oven to automatically shut off in an hour. Only twenty minutes to go.

There was a knock at the door. Her pulse raced.

In the past she might have paused, taken a moment to compose herself, not wanting to seem overeager. Now she flung open the door and graced him with a bright, welcoming smile. "You're here!"

"You're stunning." His gaze dropped over her body, then returned to her eyes. "I've never seen you in a dress before."

She couldn't suppress the audacious hope that he'd see her out of the dress later. "You look nice, too. Come on in."

With the door shut behind them, he handed her a bottle of white wine. "I stopped and got this. Shall we chill it?"

"Thank you, that was very thoughtful." She studied the label. "As it happens, this is one of my favorites."

"Oh, it isn't for you," he drawled, following her into the kitchen. "It's for me. I haven't done this in a long time, and I figured I might need liquid courage."

She laughed. "Am I that scary?"

Leaning closer, he traced his index finger down her face and over her collarbone. "Terrifying."

Shivering at his touch, she whispered, "Back at you."

As soon as she'd placed the bottle of wine in the fridge, he pulled her into his arms and kissed her thoroughly. Long, leisurely moments later, when she came up for air, Brenna purred, "I do like the way you say hi."

He kissed her again, more intensely, until throbbing need built inside her. Her knees felt shaky, and she let herself lean on him for support.

She bit her bottom lip. "It's been a long time for me, too, so I'm fuzzy on the etiquette of a date. What if, for instance, I skipped over the preliminaries and food and asked you to make love to me? Would that be moving too fast?"

"Fast?" His dark eyes blazed with intensity, his voice a rasp. "I've wanted to be inside you for days."

His raw desire for her was dizzying. "Come with me," she said.

He raised an eyebrow, a naughty grin tugging at his mouth.

She grinned back at him. "Into the living room!"

Taking her hand, he led her into the other room, kissing her again long before they ever reached the couch. When the backs of her legs bumped the cushions, she just kept going, reclining and pulling him down with her. They shifted so that he was lying next to her, partly atop her, still exchanging those soul-searing, bone-melting kisses.

"You're so good at this," she whispered, knowing instinctively that he'd be just as skilled with the rest of it.

As if reading her mind and wanting to prove her

right, he nuzzled a path of kisses down toward the cleavage of her dress, stopping only when he reached the lacy edges of her bra. Then he glanced up, locking gazes with her as he untied the straps of her dress. The material slid lazily down over her shoulders, and he sucked in a breath at the sight of her in just her bra.

He traced his thumb in a wide arc over one silky cup, and her nipples hardened into tight points. She wanted to rush him onward, needing more, even as she wanted it to take forever, drawing out the potent pleasure and the deliciously exquisite ache he created. Threading her fingers through his hair, she pulled him down for a hard kiss. He deftly unclasped her bra, baring her to his touch. Instead of feeling self-conscious, she felt wanton and decadent. When he took her in his mouth, she arched off the couch with a little cry.

His weight on top of her was thrilling, but she wanted to feel him against her, nothing separating their flesh. She skimmed her hands beneath the hem of his shirt and across the muscles of his back. He sat up, breaking their kiss long enough for her to tug the fabric up and over his head. He was even better-looking without his clothes.

She dropped her hand to the zipper of his jeans, running her palm down the length of his erection through the denim. He groaned, squeezing his eyes shut for just a moment. When he opened them again, there was such blatant hunger in them that she trembled all the way to her core. She stood, giving her sundress one solid pull and letting it pool at her feet. Never once taking his eyes off her, Adam removed the rest of his clothes.

She straddled him, moving against his lap, their mouths fused together. His tongue thrust against hers, stoking an already out-of-control need. She shimmied out of her panties while he fumbled for a condom. Then she raised herself over him and slowly eased down, gasping at the erotic shock of him inside her. For a second she went completely still, savoring the feel of their joined bodies. But then he brushed his thumbs over her nipples, lightly at first, then with increasing pressure. She tightened around him, her body moving of its own accord.

Keeping his eyes on hers, he trailed his hands up her thighs, unerringly finding where she was most sensitive. The combination of sensations was overwhelming, hurtling her toward climax. He gripped her hips and drove up into her, relentlessly pushing her over the edge.

"Adam!" She felt flung from her body, distantly aware of him finding his own release. Incapable of thought, she sagged against his chest, bonelessly content. *A girl could get used to this.*

It was a dangerous thought. Used to it? Not unless she wanted her heart broken. Because he was leaving in five days.

He stroked her hair. "That…"

"Yeah."

For a long time it was the most coherent speech they could manage. Reverently he laid her back, easing her onto the couch and covering her with his big body. He felt so good above her that she decided she wanted to make love this way the next time. Because they were *definitely* doing that again. There were so many things she wanted to do with this man, say to him, share with him. Realizing just how limited her opportunities were left a cold knot of dread in her chest.

"When do you have to go?" she asked. Did she sound panicky?

"In a hurry to get rid of me?" he drawled.

She dredged up enough energy to thump him on the back.

He kissed her collarbone, and she could feel him smile against her. "It's okay, we still have time."

No. We don't.

"I DON'T WANT to go," Adam said mournfully.

The sheet slid across Brenna's naked skin as she sat up to hug him. "I know. But you have to."

She needed him to go, anyway. She'd shuffled some appointments around to have tonight free, and tomorrow would start even earlier than usual. Yet she wondered now if she would have difficulty falling asleep. Her bed, which had always been more than adequate, was going to seem annoyingly empty once he departed.

He turned, covering her hand with his. "I wanted to ask you a favor."

"Well, now would be the perfect time to do it," she

said wryly. After experiencing three shattering orgasms tonight, she was inclined to give him whatever he asked.

"Spend the Fourth of July with us?"

She wasn't sure what she'd expected to hear, but that hadn't been it. The invitation was...sweet. "It's my busiest day this week, Adam. I'd love to, I would, but I can't."

His face fell. "We leave very early on the sixth. I won't be here much longer."

She tried to smile, but it felt so forced that she turned and rested her head against his broad shoulder, where he couldn't see her expression. "We'll always have Mistletoe," she quipped.

"And that's enough for you?" He didn't sound accusing, but was genuinely bewildered.

"It has to be enough." She pulled away and scooted up alongside him. Accepting reality was easier when they weren't touching. "Adam, let's look at this pragmatically. You have those three wonderful children who need you and an all-consuming job. I have a life here in Mistletoe and a business I'm trying to build.

"I'm so glad I met you I wouldn't trade tonight for anything. But do you honestly see this having some sort of long-distance future?"

"I... With my career, that is hard to imagine," he admitted.

"And do you see yourself moving to Mistletoe?"

"Away from my kids? Of course not!"

"Which is as it should be. By the same token, I've

worked to establish a solid reputation and enough word of mouth to sustain a client base. I'm not going anywhere. I'd have to start completely over and I spent the first half of my life doing that. This—us—was temporary." Her voice softened. "Incredible and something I'll always remember. But temporary."

"I know you're right." He cupped her cheek. "But I selfishly want more of you before I go. You've come to mean a lot to the kids, too. Are you sure you can't join us? If not for the downtown festival during the day, at least for the fireworks?"

"I don't know. I'm booked solid. By the time I finish daytime assignments, I'll barely have time to grab something to eat before it's time to get the evening visits started. But maybe," she mused, tamping down the objections of her own common sense, "with careful scheduling and some help…"

There were several subdivisions where she had more than one customer on the same street, the beauty of happy pet-owners referring their neighbors to her. If Quinn was willing to help, could they set up a divide-and-conquer system? The woman had ridden with Brenna a couple of times in the past, learning the ropes. Would she be ready for a couple of the simpler solo gigs?

Brenna had known that, by the winter holidays, she didn't want to be working alone. She'd warned her clients already that she might occasionally bring in someone else for training purposes or give someone working for her temporary use of a house key. Her customers trusted her and agreed that, at her discretion, she could send an employee on her behalf.

"I'll look into it," Brenna said. "But no promises, so don't get too attached to the idea."

He gave her a rueful smile. "A little late for that warning. I'm already too attached."

Chapter Fourteen

Adam was relieved that none of the kids asked for details of his date the next day. He wasn't sure what he would have said. Mostly they chatted about the upcoming festival. Josh had told Geoff all about the annual antique car show that the boy was excited about, while Morgan looked forward to the fireworks. If Eliza seemed less ebullient about the event than her siblings, at least she wasn't being negative about it.

"Daddy," Morgan asked during lunch, "can Brenna come with us to the festival?"

Adam grinned. "Great minds think alike."

Morgan wrinkled her nose. "What's that mean?"

"It means I already asked her," he said. Seeing the excitement lighting his daughter's eyes, he hastened to add, "But she probably won't be able to."

Eliza looked sullen, but he couldn't tell whether his daughter was miffed that he'd invited Brenna or upset that the woman wouldn't be able to come with them.

"She really *wants* to come with us," he assured

Morgan, "but she has a lot of work to do that day. It depends on whether she can find help with her pet-sitting."

"I'll help!" the five-year-old declared.

Geoff laughed. "Spending the day with dogs and kitty cats does sound right up your alley, but we can't. Brenna told me that only adults are allowed to go into the houses where she's working."

Morgan scowled, but seemed unwilling to let the matter go. "Daddy's an adult. He could help."

Eliza exhaled impatiently. "Then what do *we* do, dummy?"

"That's not how we talk to one another," Adam reprimanded sternly.

Geoff's expression was thoughtful. "I don't know, I think the squirt's on to something. What if we could hang out at the festival with Josh and Natalie? Then Dad and Brenna could meet us there later, like, for dinner and stuff. They might miss some of it, but the fireworks are the coolest part, anyway. We like Josh and Natalie, right?"

"Right!" Morgan chirped.

Even Eliza was forced to admit, "They're pretty cool. For grown-ups."

"I don't know." Adam hesitated. Josh and Natalie had already been very gracious with their time, and he didn't want to take advantage of their generosity. Besides, it had never been his intention to spend the holiday away from his children.

Still, time with Brenna was running out fast. They had only a few days left together, and he couldn't deny wanting to steal as many moments and memories as possible before his vacation was done.

When Brenna's cell phone rang that night, she knew instinctively that it would be Adam. Though she hadn't realized it until now, she'd been waiting for him to call.

"Hi," he said. "Got a minute to talk?"

"I can spare a minute." *For you.* "I might even have some good news. Quinn said she'd help me on the Fourth. It will still be awfully tight, but if I push—"

"As it turns out, I have a little good news myself. How would you feel about an extra pair of hands? I don't know the area well enough to be zigzagging around town on my own, and people here don't know me at all, but could I help if I rode with you?"

Yes, actually. There were always several small tasks to do at each stop, and two could work faster than one. Her heart sped up. The idea of hours alone with Adam seemed like a precious gift. She wasn't in danger of falling into the habit of leaning on him. He wouldn't be around long enough for that to happen.

"What about the kids?" she asked.

"Well, Geoff tossed out the idea that maybe they could hang with your brother. If you don't think he's sick of them?"

"Oh, he's crazy about them. But I know he's working some of the midway games, and Natalie's busy with the parade that morning. I tell you what—let me talk to them and determine everyone's schedule."

"Meanwhile, I'll talk to Lydia," he brainstormed. "But if we can work it out, you'll let me come with you? I really want to help."

"And I really appreciate it," she said softly, but she was torn between being overjoyed by his offer and wishing he hadn't called.

If she kept falling for Adam Varner, who was going to help her recover when he left town and broke her heart?

As IT TURNED OUT, finding a babysitter for the festival was easy. Maggie called Brenna's cell phone early Wednesday morning to ask if she wanted to bring her new friend to Sunday dinner.

"I don't know," Brenna said. "I'll definitely pass along the invitation, but it will be up to the Varners. Sunday is their last evening here, and I'm not sure what they have planned."

"I suppose that's understandable." Maggie sounded disappointed. "We were just hoping to meet him. And those kids! Seems like a lifetime ago that you and Josh were young."

An idea took shape in Brenna's mind. After all, who was better with children than Maggie Pierce? "Hey, are you guys going to the festival this year?"

"Of course! You know Fred never misses the turtle race. He won't admit it, but I'm pretty sure he bets on those silly races every year."

Most men did, even if they felt foolish owning up to it—it was a Mistletoe tradition.

"This may be a lot to ask, but how would you feel about some extra company for the festival?"

IT WAS BARELY FIVE in the morning when Brenna got out of bed on Independence Day. She'd spoken with Quinn and Adam multiple times in preparation. Since she couldn't in good conscience inflict this early hour on either of them, she'd decided to do the first visits by herself and then meet up with them at the Diner for a quick breakfast while she divvied up everyone's duties for the day.

She caught herself humming as she cleaned a fish tank. Though she liked her job, she wasn't usually *this* peppy first thing in the morning. She shied away from admitting to herself just how much she was looking forward to seeing him.

Quinn, however, was unashamed of her own eager curiosity to meet him. She called Brenna to let her know she was en route to the Diner. "I can't wait to see this guy! I hate that I was out of town the night of your date—you know, the one you refuse to share any of the details about. I would have been happy to give you wardrobe advice."

Brenna grinned into the receiver, glad her friend couldn't see her telltale smirk. "Oh, I did all right on my own."

"If I get there first, do you want me to order for you?" Quinn offered.

"Yes, please. I have to walk the Webers' Weimaraner, but then I'm on my way." She'd just given Quinn her breakfast request and disconnected when the phone chirped again. "Hello?"

"Morning." Adam's voice rumbled through the phone.

She felt her entire body responding, her face smiling, her posture subtly relaxing. "Hey, there. Maggie make it over to the lodge?"

"Oh, yes." The two words held a wealth of humor. "She's quite…I think she hugged me three times. And she managed to carry on concurrent conversations with Geoff about the car show today, Eliza about some new brand of lip gloss and Morgan about her favorite cartoon. How does Maggie even know about *that?*"

"Neighborhood kids, I imagine. It started when a girl across the street would come over for the time between when she got home from school and when her mother got home from her part-time job. She'd hang out in Maggie's kitchen. Word about the pie got out, and now there's at least one kid dropping by every day of the week. Maggie's good with them."

"I'll say! I got tired just listening to her chat with my three."

Brenna laughed. "Not too tired, I hope. I plan to work you hard today."

There was a pregnant pause.

"Adam! You're awful."

"What? I didn't say anything. Don't project your wicked thoughts onto *me.*"

She was grinning from ear to ear when they got off the phone. The sun was shining, the kids were in great hands, her good friend promised to have caffeine ready and waiting, and Brenna would get to spend hours alone with Adam, culminating in brilliant fireworks.

It was going to be a great day.

BY MIDMORNING Brenna and Adam had fallen into an easy, natural rhythm. While they were driving, they chatted and laughed a lot. She learned that the Rolling Stones were his favorite band and that he did a truly terrible Mick Jagger impression. She'd written a list of their assignments, analyzing location and meds schedules to put them in the order that made the most sense. After each visit was concluded and she'd double-checked that the house was secure, they'd return to the car where he'd immediately read off the next stop.

In the car, she'd outline what she needed him to do. Usually he handled stuff like bringing in people's mail and watering plants while she took care of the pets. At one house, he tossed a tennis ball in the backyard for an indefatigable Jack Russell terrier while Brenna filled food bowls and undertook the always fun mission of giving a cat a pill. While Adam's presence only shaved off a few minutes at most visits, those minutes added up over the course of the day. As soon as they reached their destination, chitchat stopped as they focused on their respective tasks.

She pulled into a driveway in the Heritage Pond subdivision, and he had his seat belt off before she got her keys out of the ignition.

"Synchronize watches," he deadpanned. "And we're ready to move out. Go, go, go, this is *not* a drill!"

Once they met back up at the front door to leave the house, she asked, "Do your patients know the truth about you, that you're a total nut?"

"No, the hospital's worked very hard to keep that under wraps. Otherwise people tend not to trust me with cutting their chests open."

She shuddered. "The less time I spend thinking about what you actually do, the better. I couldn't take it, the pressure of essentially holding someone else's heart in my hands."

He paused in the act of opening the passenger door, giving her a long, measured look over the roof of the hatchback.

Brenna swallowed. She'd never really wanted to be entrusted with someone else's heart, but the thought of Adam putting such faith in her was both humbling and intoxicating.

Why now? She blinked rapidly, hoping he didn't notice as they climbed into the car. *Why did it have to be you?* Yet she couldn't find it in herself to regret anything that had transpired between them.

They hadn't made it out of the subdivision before her cell phone rang. Quinn, she figured. Her friend should be about done with her short list of assignments; she had others that had to wait until this evening. She was probably calling to check in.

"More than Pup—" Brenna broke off, realizing that a phone was still ringing.

Adam had simultaneously realized the same thing. "Hello? Geoff, I don't… Slow down. Maggie's giving what to who?"

Gripped by a sense of foreboding, Brenna diverted her attention from the road to Adam's profile. He'd gone ashen.

"We'll be right there." He snapped the phone closed. "We need to get to the festival. Now. Morgan's missing."

THOUGH BRENNA had turned around immediately, she'd been heading in the opposite direction of the festival. It would take them at least fifteen minutes to get there, and she'd been hoping with every fiber of her body that Maggie would have called by the time they arrived to let them know the little girl had been discovered safe and sound.

But that was not the case.

The festival was sprawled over the entire area of Mistletoe's quaint downtown. There was not one main entry point. You simply parked in a field or lot as close as you could get, then walked from there. Maggie had been with the kids on the parade route while Fred had gone to buy them cold beverages—the temperature had already been well into the nineties by the time the parade started.

According to Geoff, one minute Morgan had been standing with them among the throng on the sidewalk, the next she'd been gone. In the dense crowd it had been difficult to spot someone so small. As soon as they'd realized what had happened, Maggie had given the little girl's description to nearby police officers while Geoff called his dad.

Adam hadn't said anything the entire ride, and Brenna couldn't think of what to say to him other than a firm "We'll find her." He'd nodded tersely, his jaw clenched.

When River had been a kitten, she'd slid out the door without Brenna noticing and hadn't come home for nearly two days. Brenna had been beside herself with worry. And that was a *cat.* She couldn't imagine the hell Adam was going through imagining his five-year-old daughter scared and alone in the packed streets of an unfamiliar town.

Brenna stopped the car, and Adam was out the door before she'd even put it in Park. She saw him dial his phone, heard him ask Geoff, "Anything?" and watched his shoulders sag in defeat.

There was no central PA system for the festival, but several venues used microphones, such as the local bands performing in the oversize gazebo and the sports announcers covering the turtle races. According to Geoff, Fred was systematically going to each of those places to seek people's help and to ask that anyone seeing Morgan call his cell phone number. Meanwhile, Maggie and Eliza were thoroughly checking all the women's restrooms in case Morgan had wandered off simply because she needed to go to the bathroom. They were all keeping contact via phone and had left Geoff standing on the sidewalk along the parade route—the last thing they wanted was for Morgan to return only to find everyone else gone.

Geoff described his location to his dad, and Adam turned away from the phone for a moment to ask Brenna, "You know where Christy's Crafts Corner is?" At her nod, he told his son, "Stay put, we're coming to you."

Mistletoe hosted many seasonal events, from the community haunted house every fall to the Winter Wonderland dance that benefited the seniors center. Brenna had always loved these activities, enjoyed the buzzing energy of the crowd, running into dozens of familiar acquaintances. Today, however, the sheer number of people became oppressive and sinister; what would this crush seem like to a little girl who didn't know anyone?

As they shouldered their way through the mob, Brenna offered the only support she could think of— reaching down and taking Adam's hand. He stiffened for a second, and she wondered if he would pull away. But then he squeezed her fingers.

She pointed to the left. "The craft store that Geoff's in front of is just—"

"Daddy!"

Given the high volume of ambient noise, it was amazing they even heard her, but Adam whipped around so quickly he almost took out a passing pedestrian. He scanned the crowd, relief instantly flooding his expression when he spotted his daughter a few yards away. He took off in her direction, Brenna hurrying to catch up, and dropped to his knees in front of her. Morgan looked scared, but not nearly to the degree her father had been. His entire body was shaking as he squashed her into his embrace.

"Morgan! Oh, thank God," he chanted. "Thank God, thank God. You scared the he— Where *were* you, baby?"

Her lower lip quivered, tears welling in her sky-blue eyes. "I…I don't know. I just wanted to pet the little doggie, but then…" She began to wail.

Adam scooped her up in his arms, shushing her.

"Can you give me Geoff's number? I'll call him," Brenna offered. She did so, moved by the naked relief in the teenager's voice that his sister had been found. Next, Brenna called Maggie, knowing her stepmother must be frantic with concern and guilt.

"We found her," Brenna said. "She wasn't that far from where you guys were standing. I think she followed a puppy and got too turned around to find her way back."

Adam had moved on from consoling to gently lecturing. His voice was kind but firm as he admonished Morgan to never, never, never, never do that again.

"Praise the lord," Maggie said with feeling. "Eliza and I will meet you back there. I'll call Fred now."

Brenna could hear Eliza's whoop of joy in the background as Maggie relayed the good news.

But joy was not the emotion plastered across the girl's tearstained features when she stormed up to them a few minutes later. "Morgan Renee Varner, don't you ever do that again!"

Morgan huddled shyly into her father's side. "Sorry," she mumbled.

"Eliza," Adam said, "I know how upset you—"

"This is all your fault!" the girl blasted him, narrowing red-rimmed eyes. "You swore this trip was about us, spending time with your children! Then you went and dumped us on a total stranger—"

Maggie flinched but didn't interrupt.

"—so that you could make some kind of booty call or something—"

"That is enough," Adam said, his voice soft but echoing with cold finality.

Eliza's shoulders slumped as if from the weight of all the emotions she'd gone through today. She stopped raging, but wounded anger still shadowed her gaze. "She's not even your girlfriend, Dad. But you broke your promise for her. What if something had happened to Morgan?"

Adam briefly squeezed his eyes closed, actually staggering back a step as his daughter's words struck him like a boxer's KO punch. Brenna was certain Eliza hadn't said anything he wasn't already thinking himself. More than she had ever before, Brenna wanted to reach out to another person. She wanted to hug him, soothe him with reminders that his daughter was all right now. But under the circumstances, her touching Adam right now might not be welcome.

A lump rose in Brenna's throat when Geoff, somehow looking years older than when she'd last seen him, moved closer to his father, laying a hand on his arm. An unmistakable sign of solidarity and support.

"Morgan," Geoff began kindly, "why don't you tell everyone you're sorry? Especially Maggie. She was nice enough to bring us to the festival, then you scared her to death."

"D-didn't m-mean to." Morgan hiccupped. "P-please don't f-fight."

"Nobody's fighting," Adam promised her. He shot a pointed glance at his other daughter.

Eliza nodded.

Brenna took that as her cue. "I'm so glad everyone's okay. Why don't you stick together for the rest of the day? I want you guys to have fun with your dad today at the festival." She retreated a step.

Adam raised his gaze to her, looking miserable but grateful. They both knew there was no way he could go back to helping her with pet assignments now, and she was officially behind schedule. The way things stood, it was better that she didn't intrude by joining them for fireworks.

She turned to Maggie, who was wringing her hands. "Adam and I both appreciate your doing us the favor. I'm sure the kids were having a great time earlier. I'll see you for Sunday dinner?"

Her stepmother nodded, and Brenna kissed her on the cheek.

"And I'll see *you*," Brenna told the Varners, not quite meeting Adam's eyes, "the day after tomorrow. You can stop by and pick up Ellie on your way out of town." It was hard to get those words past the growing lump.

"Brenna." The way he said her name was an ache.

She refuted him with a quick toss of her head. She wouldn't, couldn't, do the painfully drawn-out, emotional goodbye. *That's why Mom left the way she did,* she realized suddenly. In retrospect, it had probably been better for both of them. If Brenna had known what her mother was planning to do, there would have been tears. She would have clung to her, begged her not to go.

Deep down, part of Brenna was having that same reaction to Adam now. *Don't go.* Which was stupid, of course, but she couldn't completely silence the inner plea.

Chapter Fifteen

Brenna opened her front door when she heard the tires in the driveway, resolved to be strong. Adam had called her last night to make sure she wouldn't be flitting off to her first morning assignments before they got there.

"You will *be there, right?"*

Was it her imagination, or had there been an implied threat in his tone—as if he contemplated hunting her down if she tried to duck out of the farewell? He'd immediately seized the advantage when she hesitated, claiming that the kids deserved the chance for a face-to-face goodbye and that she should understand that better than anyone. Dirty pool, in Brenna's opinion.

But despite the attractive draw of the coward's way out, Brenna couldn't do it. Not only did she owe the kids a goodbye, she owed it to herself.

Well, here's your chance.

Her eyes burned but remained dry as she watched the Varners file out of the SUV. At dinner last night,

Maggie had confided that Adam had called her yesterday, asking if he and the kids could buy the Pierces lunch at the Diner. It was clear he wanted to make amends for what had happened and demonstrate that he didn't blame Maggie in the least.

"We actually had a pretty good time," Maggie said sorrowfully. "They're a really nice family. Even that Eliza, when you get beneath the anger and pubescent mood swings. She'll grow out of that."

As usual, Brenna's stepmom was right. They *were* a great family, and Brenna would miss each and every one of them. Even Eliza.

"Brenna!" Morgan squealed, restored to her usual exuberance since the last time they'd seen each other.

Brenna came down the porch steps to hug her. "Ready to take Ellie home and show her Tennessee?"

"Yep! Dad says we can pick out more stuff for her once we get her to his place. I made you a thank-you card for taking care of her." Morgan handed her a folded piece of paper with crayon renditions of herself, Brenna and the cat.

"Thank *you*. This means a lot to me." *I am* not *going to cry.*

Geoff was next. "It was nice to meet you. We had a great vacation."

But now it was time for all of them to return to the real world.

She squeezed his shoulder. "Thanks for your help with my taxes."

He winked at her, and she had a premonition of him as a grown man. "Try not to get audited."

Adam cleared his throat. "Geoff and I are going to get Ellie's stuff and load it into the car. If that's okay?"

Brenna nodded, choking on everything she wanted to say to him. Even though no part of him brushed her as he passed—he gave her an unnecessarily wide berth—she felt his nearness as tangibly as a touch. The boys went inside, and Morgan asked permission to go pet Zoe and River one last time.

"Yes," Brenna said, "but you have to promise me you'll never follow another animal away from your parents or brother or sister or caregiver. It's not safe. People need to know where you are, and you shouldn't approach strange animals, anyway."

Morgan hung her head. "I know. I told everyone I was really, really sorry." Suitably reprimanded, she slunk into the house.

Leaving only Eliza, who sat on the hood of the car, picking at her nails. She'd chipped the hell out of her manicure.

Brenna sat next to her. "I know you don't want to talk to me, but humor me. One last girl-to-girl." First their chat about boys on the sunporch, then the crash course on pads, tampons and the most effective way to treat menstrual cramps. *I'm having quite the Dear Abby summer.*

Would the third time be the charm? She hoped that the girl was open-minded enough to truly hear what

Brenna had to say. Since Brenna would probably never see the Varners again, she stood to gain nothing by this, but if a brief chat could make any improvement in Eliza's life or Adam's…

"I get why you were mad at your father the other day, but try to cut him some slack. When you guys get back home to Knoxville, don't bust his chops every time he asks out a woman."

Eliza remained mutinously silent.

"Seriously, you stand to benefit from your dad finding romance. Love isn't finite. That's something I didn't realize at your age." She recalled how worried she'd been that Fred and Maggie might not have enough parental affection to go around for their natural child *and* Brenna.

"Loving someone teaches you to have a bigger heart, makes you more likely to be patient and demonstrative with everyone else in your life. I know *I'm* better off for having fallen in love with—" She stopped abruptly, appalled at what she'd been about to say. "I'm better off." Best to leave it at that.

Eliza finally looked up. "You don't hate me?"

"Oh, honey." If Brenna couldn't understand a kid bitter about potentially losing a parent, who could? Just because Eliza was dead wrong about Adam—he would never willingly leave these kids—didn't make her pain any less real. "I don't hate you."

"I know I've been a little…grumpy."

Brenna managed a grin. "We've all been there. Let she who is without PMS cast the first stone."

Eliza laughed. On the steps to the house, Geoff and Adam both froze at the musical sound.

"Whoa," Geoff said to his father. "How did Brenna do that?"

Adam shrugged, but the ghost of a smile played about his lips. "She must have mad skills."

Geoff groaned. "Don't say stuff like that, Dad, I beg you."

Though Eliza could no doubt hear them just as well as Brenna could, she ignored them. Instead, she frowned thoughtfully at Brenna. "You know, I think my mom would really like you."

Once the kids and cat were packed into the car, Adam came toward her. Her heart hammered in her chest. She felt like she was dying for him to kiss her goodbye but risked dying a little inside if he did. Better to keep a safe distance, she told herself. Then she gave herself a shake. Her entire life, she'd subconsciously tried to keep people at a safe distance.

Until Adam and his kids.

Even with as much pain as she felt now, she was glad she'd met them, glad she'd been with him. In that spirit, she marched forward and clutched his shirtfront as she rose on her toes and planted one last kiss on his lips.

He clearly hadn't expected that. His eyes were wide when she backed away. "I won't ever meet another woman quite like you."

"Safe journeys, Adam. Take care of your kids."

"Take care of yourself," he told her.

Those damn tears tried to rise again. "I always do."

He got in the car and after one final, lingering look, gunned the engine and backed out of the driveway. She shaded her eyes against the sun and watched the SUV's progress up and over the hill. Adam Varner was gone from her life just as he'd driven into it.

THE TRIP TO Knoxville wasn't bad as far as road trips with three kids went. There was minimal yowling from a crated Ellie, punctuated by isolated squabbles. But none of that was as bad as Adam's hollow feeling, as if he'd left part of himself in Mistletoe. Namely, his heart.

Luckily the kids all seemed to be in high spirits, excited to tell their mom and friends all about their vacation, so he tried to use that to bolster his own mood. It worked mostly, right up until the time they passed the Welcome to Tennessee sign and Eliza burst into tears.

"What now," Geoff muttered, rolling his eyes in the front seat.

Eliza didn't seem to notice. "You were right, Dad. I *am* a selfish brat!"

"Uh…" Adam searched his memory bank. "I'm pretty sure I didn't say that." Had he? Sara would kill him. He was pretty sure name-calling fell under the heading of Bad Parenting.

But then, so did losing your youngest child.

"At Kerrigan Farms," Eliza insisted. "It's what you said, more or less."

"I think sometimes you can act selfishly," he said, choosing his words carefully. "The same is true of everyone. Work harder to make good choices, and take other people's feelings into consideration. What is this about, Liza?"

"Your feelings. And Ms. Pierce's. I was so upset when Bobby liked that other girl."

Bobby the punk lifeguard? Adam waited, not sure where his daughter was going with her line of reasoning. Assuming there was one.

"But you must feel a billion times worse leaving Brenna! I never should have yelled at the two of you."

"I agree that you overreacted the other day, and if you're feeling badly about what you said, maybe you could send her a note of apology. But don't beat yourself up too much. We were always going to leave Mistletoe. Brenna knew that." Had seemed to accept it more easily than he had, as a matter-of-fact. "We never had a real future."

"But she *loves* you," Eliza sobbed. "I messed up everything! You could have been happy, like Mom and Dan."

His mind flashed to Sara and Dan's wedding, only it was himself he pictured, Brenna's face beneath the ivory veil. And it was all too easy to picture the two of them away on a tropical honeymoon.

"Let's not blow everything out of proportion," he

said, his caution more for himself than his daughter. "Brenna cared about me, she cared about all of us, but 'love' is a strong—"

"I'm not being melodramatic! She *said* it this morning. She said she loved you and was a better person because of it."

Adam's heartbeat exploded in his ears. For a second he felt so dizzy he worried about driving safely. Taking a deep breath, he maneuvered the car over to the shoulder of the road.

"You're sure?" he asked his daughter. He had difficulty letting himself believe it, but maybe it wasn't so farfetched.

After all, *he'd* fallen in love with *her*.

"Eliza, what else did she say?"

BRENNA SAT with Quinn and Arianne Waide on Quinn's front porch, battling the suspicion that she'd been invited to their girls' night because Quinn felt sorry for her. But coming here to vent over margaritas had sounded a damn sight better than staying home and wallowing. Since the clients who'd scheduled their vacation to coincide with the Fourth of July were home now, she didn't even have a busy work schedule to take her mind off things.

Things? Way to deflect, Bren. There was only one "thing" on her mind. Dr. Adam Varner.

"We've lost her," Ari told Quinn in a mock whisper.

"Thinking about the handsome doc again?" Quinn asked sympathetically.

"Yes." There was no point in denying it.

Ari ran her finger around the rim of her glass, bringing the salt to her lips. "I'm sorry I never got to meet him. Our entire family has been so wrapped up with the new baby. Was the surgeon really that hot?"

"Yes," Quinn and Brenna chorused.

Brenna raised her eyebrows.

Quinn chuckled. "Well, he was."

"These summer-lovin' flings never end well," Ari said, the sage tone a bit humorous coming from a twenty-three-year-old. "*Grease* being the exception that proves the rule."

"The worst part is he was a good guy," Quinn said. "If he had any decency, he would have done something hateful so we could sit here and bash him, which might make you feel better, Brenna."

"No, I knew from day one that he would be leaving. And I knew his kids needed to be his top priority. That's one of the things I admired about him even."

Quinn shrugged. "Then I'm afraid all I've got is the chestnut about it being better to have loved and lost than to—"

"Oh, please!" Arianne was aghast. "I always thought that dumb saying applied only to wimpy women. I say if you love them, track their butts down."

Quinn looked equal parts fascinated and horrified. "Ari, I think any guy you ever set your sights on should be a little afraid."

Tuning out their banter, Brenna allowed herself to

consider, just for a second, what "tracking him down" would entail. A long-distance relationship? To what end? Even if she thought they were suited to that—and she suspected she wasn't, while he'd flat-out said he didn't want that—where would it lead? The more time she spent in Mistletoe, the deeper the roots of her company. Besides, as she'd learned after going away to college, this was home. She'd gone too long without one to give it up lightly. Whereas Adam had a cardiac practice and the three most important people in the world to him grounding him in Knoxville.

No, it was best that they'd parted ways cleanly. The most she could do now was try to learn from what happened between them. Maybe, eventually, she could honor her feelings for him by being more open to relationships in the future. Unfortunately, as hard as she tried, she couldn't imagine being happy with a "next" guy. Her heart already knew the guy it wanted.

SARA INSISTED that Adam at least stay for dinner before heading home. "You've been on the road for hours. Stay, please."

The kids had enthusiastically cheered this idea, so he'd capitulated. He couldn't get that excited about going home to his empty place, anyway. He found himself absurdly grateful for the cat. She would help mitigate the solitude—plus, she was a reminder of Brenna. After dinner Geoff disappeared into his room to call Gina,

Eliza booted up her computer to message her friends and Dan went to tuck in a very tired Morgan.

"So." Sara propped an elbow on the table, leaning her chin on her fist. "Some trip, huh?"

"I am so sorry about Morgan getting lost like that. I swear I—"

"Adam. I don't blame you for that. We've never endured anything on quite that scale, but there have been moments. Do you remember when Eliza was about her age and I told you how much I panicked when I looked around a department store and didn't see her?"

He was startled. "No." That seemed like something he *should* remember.

"Oh. Well, it turned out she thought it would be funny to play hide-and-seek and had dropped to the floor, crawling into a rack of clothes. She was only gone for a minute or two before I realized what had happened, but for that minute..."

"Thank you." After all the times he'd given Sara reason to be frustrated with his parenting efforts, or lack thereof, he deeply appreciated her trying to make him feel like he was a good father.

She suddenly grinned, mischievous. "I want to hear more about this Brenna."

His face actually warmed. *Oh, brother.* Was he blushing in front of his ex? He'd managed to head off the moment at dinner when Eliza had started to share that Brenna "loved" him, but he hadn't done so quickly or gracefully enough to deter Sara's interest.

What the hell, he might as well tell her about Brenna. If he didn't, she'd hear all about her from the kids, anyway.

"She's amazing. It's like she gave everyone exactly what they needed. A cat for Morgan, the pride of employee responsibility for Geoff, womanly advice for Eliza—just until we were able to get you on the phone," he added quickly.

"What about you? What did she give you that you needed?"

He was quiet for so long that even he didn't think he would answer the question until he heard himself say, "Love. It sounds insane, doesn't it? But I think I love her."

Sara straightened. "Then what are you doing *here?*"

"What do you mean?"

"You're in love with a woman in Mistletoe, Georgia."

"Yes." Funny, but the more times he admitted it, the better he felt.

"Then either she needs to be here or you need to be there. Adam, no offense, but I've watched you squander love before. The kids', before you finally wised up— this vacation was the smartest thing you've done in years—mine." She held up a hand, fending him off. "I'm not blaming you for the divorce. We both could have done things differently. But people loved you."

"And I took it for granted," he said softly. After this past week he truly believed that he and the kids were on the right track again. But how much time had he lost?

He thought of Brenna and considered Sara's de-

ceptively simple question: *What are you doing here?*
Did he want to lose any more time with someone he
loved, or seize the day and be with her?

SINCE BRENNA HADN'T been sleeping well for the past
week and a half, it seemed likely that the SUV sitting
in her driveway was a hallucination born of exhaustion.
She rubbed her eyes and looked again.

Still there.

By the time she'd parked behind it, she'd already
seen the man sitting at the top step of her porch. *Adam!*
She was completely flummoxed, her shock not fading
in the slightest as she got out of the car and approached
him with no clue what to say.

"What are you *doing* here?"

He leaned back on his elbows and grinned. "I get
that a lot. You look good."

Then he must be even more tired than she was.
She'd overslept this morning and dressed without a
shower, slapping a ball cap on her head and vowing to
come home and clean up more when she was done
with the visits that had to be taken care of early. She
certainly hadn't expected to find Adam sitting here
when she returned.

"How long have you been waiting?" she asked.

"Since about seven-thirty. I brought two cups of
coffee, hoping to catch you before you started your day.
I wound up drinking them both," he said sheepishly.

"B-but what if I hadn't come home between morning and midday assignments? You weren't really planning to sit on my porch all day?"

"Not *all* day." He gave her a lopsided smile. "I have an appointment at three."

She plopped down on the step next to him, partly because she didn't think her legs would support her anymore. This was a lot to take in. "You came back."

For her? What kind of appointment? Was he doing some sort of medical consulting here in Mistletoe?

"Had to. I forgot something." He slid closer, turning her face to meet his gaze. "I forgot to mention that I'm in love with you."

Her mind went blank. Completely and utterly void. She wasn't even sure how long she stared back at him, stupefied.

Say something, Bren! A woman more comfortable with emotional declarations would probably say she loved him, too.

Brenna, on the other hand, told him he was crazy. "In love? But that's nuts. I'm... You... What about your kids?"

"Actually, I think my improving relationship with them has made it easier to accept falling for you. As it turns out, loving someone just makes you more receptive to giving and accepting love from others. It makes you a better person."

She blinked, hearing her own words coming back to her. "Your twelve-year-old has a big mouth."

"And a big heart. She already loves you a little. And

I love you a lot." For a moment his smile slipped, vulnerability leaking into his expression. "But I should probably stop beating you over the head with declarations I'm not even sure you want to hear. You haven't mentioned whether…"

Oh, God, hadn't she said it yet? It was so ever present in her thoughts that she was surprised people couldn't look at her and *hear* her thinking it.

"I love you, Adam. I can't believe you came back for me!" When had she started crying?

He kissed her with slow thoroughness. She recalled how rushed they'd been with each other the night they'd made love, because they'd known they didn't have long. Now his every unhurried caress spoke of a man who believed they had a future.

"I've thought about you, too," she admitted, tilting into his touch as he wiped away a tear with his thumb. "I even entertained mad ideas about moving to Tennessee. But—"

"Lord, don't do that. It would be pointless if you moved there and I got a job here. Very O. Henry."

"You're applying for a job here?" she said, certain she hadn't heard him right.

He shrugged. "Why not? I care about what I do, but it doesn't have to be in Tennessee. People in Mistletoe have hearts, too."

She could attest to that. Hers was currently full to bursting.

"The medical center is attracting all kinds of new

patients, and the local hospital is going to need to take on new doctors to keep up with the growing number of surgeries. I don't think it will keep me as busy as my current position in Knoxville, but I *want* more time for me. For my kids." He stared into her eyes. "For us. Our relationship would have to be long-distance for at least a few weeks, while I get everything settled, but the people I've talked to seem very interested in signing me on."

She resisted the urge to succumb to the pure, shimmering happiness threatening to engulf her, afraid there must be some kind of catch. Not even Maggie and Fred and Josh opening their hearts to her had quite prepared her for someone loving her on a scale of this magnitude. "But how would the kids feel about it? You just said your relationship is improving, so—"

"I didn't do this without giving it serious thought," he vowed. "If that were the case, I would have been back the same night as the day I left. I talked to the kids, talked to Sara, and what we decided is this— when you love people enough, you make them part of your life. You make an effort in spite of geography. Conversely, when you're not trying, not even living under the same roof is a guarantee of being close.

"The kids don't live with me, anyway. I get them for special occasions and some weekends, which they voted unanimously that they'd be happy to spend here. Knoxville is not at the other end of the galaxy. I can—

I *will*—get up there for birthdays and graduations and school plays."

Just like that, the dam broke. The joy she hadn't quite dared to feel rushed over her in a wave and she was more than happy to let the undertow drag her out over her head. *I love you, I love you, I love you.*

She stood. "I have more pet visits to do."

He nodded, looking disappointed but trying to hide it. "I understand. Maybe—"

"But I need to shower first. You know—" she tapped her finger to her lips "—we never really got to have our date on the Fourth of July."

He arched an eyebrow. "No, I guess not."

She pushed open her front door, grinning over her shoulder. "Come on, Dr. Varner. I owe you some fireworks."

* * * * *

*There's one more season
to experience in Mistletoe, Georgia.
Look for Arianne Waide's and
Gabe Sloan's story, MISTLETOE HERO,
coming October 2009, only from
Harlequin American Romance.*

Rick's appointment with his attorney early Wednesday morning went only moderately better than his meeting with social services the day before. The prognosis wasn't great—but at least his attorney was going to file a motion for DNA testing. Just so Rick could petition to see the child…his sister's baby. The sister he didn't know he had until it was too late.

The rest of what his attorney said had been downhill from there.

Cell phone in hand before he'd even reached his Nitro, Rick punched in the speed dial number he'd programmed the day before.

Maybe foster parent Sue Bookman hadn't received his message. Or had lost his number. Maybe she didn't want to talk to him. At this point he didn't much care what she wanted.

"Hello?" She answered before the first ring was complete. And sounded breathless.

Young and breathless.

"Ms. Bookman?"

"Yes. This is Rick Kraynick, right?"

"Yes, ma'am."

"I recognized your number on caller ID," she said, her voice uneven, as though she was still engaged in whatever physical activity had her so breathless to begin with. "I'm sorry I didn't get back to you. I've been a little…distracted."

The words came in more disjointed spurts. Was she jogging?

"No problem," he said, when, in fact, he'd spent the better part of the night before watching his phone. And fretting. "Did I get you at a bad time?"

"No worse than usual," she said, adding, "Better than some. So, how can I help?"

God, if only this could be so easy. He'd ask. She'd help. And life could go well. At least for one little person in his family.

It would be a first.

"Mr. Kraynick?"

"Yes. Sorry. I was…are you sure there isn't a better time to call?"

"I'm bouncing a baby, Mr. Kraynick. It's what I do."

"Is it Carrie?" he asked quickly, his pulse racing.

"How do you know Carrie?" She sounded defensive, which wouldn't do him any good.

"I'm her uncle," he explained, "her mother's— Christy's—older brother, and I know you have her."

"I can neither confirm nor deny your allegations,

Mr. Kraynick. Please call social services." She rattled off the number.

"Wait!" he said, unable to hide his urgency. "Please," he said more calmly. "Just hear me out."

"How did you find me?"

"A friend of Christy's."

"I'm sorry I can't help you, Mr. Kraynick," she said softly. "This conversation is over."

"I grew up in foster care," he said, as though that gave him some special privilege. Some insider's edge.

"Then you know you shouldn't be calling me at all."

"Yes... But Carrie is my niece," he said. "I need to see her. To know that she's okay."

"You'll have to go through social services to arrange that."

"I'm sure you know it's not as easy as it sounds. I'm a single man with no real ties and I've no intention of petitioning for custody. They aren't real eager to give me the time of day. I never even knew Carrie's mother. For all intents and purposes, our mother didn't raise either one of us. All I have going for me is half a set of genes. My lawyer's on it, but it could be weeks— months—before this is sorted out. Carrie could be adopted by then. Which would be fine, great for her, but then I'd have lost my chance. I don't want to take her. I won't hurt her. I just have to see her."

"I'm sorry, Mr. Kraynick, but..."

* * * * *

*Find out if Rick Kraynick will ever have
a chance to meet his niece.
Look for A DAUGHTER'S TRUST
by Tara Taylor Quinn,
available in September 2009.*

We'll be spotlighting a different series
every month throughout 2009
to celebrate our 60th anniversary.

**Look for Harlequin® Superromance®
in September!**

*Celebrate with
The Diamond Legacy
miniseries!*

Follow the stories of four cousins as they come to terms
with the complications of love and what it means to
be a family. Discover with them the sixty-year-old secret
that rocks not one but two families.

A DAUGHTER'S TRUST by *Tara Taylor Quinn*
September

FOR THE LOVE OF FAMILY by *Kathleen O'Brien*
October

LIKE FATHER, LIKE SON by *Karina Bliss*
November

A MOTHER'S SECRET by *Janice Kay Johnson*
December

Available wherever books are sold.

You're invited to join our Tell Harlequin Reader Panel!

By joining our new reader panel you will:

- Receive Harlequin® books—they are FREE and yours to keep with no obligation to purchase anything!
- Participate in fun online surveys
- Exchange opinions and ideas with women just like you
- Have a say in our new book ideas and help us publish the best in women's fiction

In addition, you will have a chance to win great prizes and receive special gifts! See Web site for details. Some conditions apply. Space is limited.

To join, visit us at
www.TellHarlequin.com.

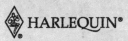

REQUEST YOUR FREE BOOKS!
2 FREE NOVELS PLUS 2
FREE GIFTS!

Love, Home & Happiness!

In 2009 Harlequin celebrates
60 years of pure reading pleasure!

We're marking this occasion by offering
16 **FREE** full books to download and read.

Visit
www.HarlequinCelebrates.com

to choose from a variety of
great romance stories
that are absolutely **FREE!**

(Total approximate retail value of $60)

We invite you to visit and share the Web site
with your friends, family
and anyone who enjoys reading.

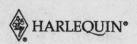

HARLEQUIN®

American ★ Romance®

COMING NEXT MONTH
Available September 8, 2009

#1273 DOCTOR DADDY by Jacqueline Diamond
Men Made in America
Dr. Jane McKay wants a child more than anything, but her dreams
of parenthood don't include the sexy, maddening doctor next door.
Luke Van Dam is *not* ready to settle down. Yet the gorgeous babe magnet
seems to attract *babies*, too—he's just become guardian of an infant girl.
Is Luke the right man to share Jane's dream after all?

#1274 ONCE A COP by Lisa Childs
Citizen's Police Academy
Roberta "Robbie" Meyers wants a promotion out of the Lakewood P.D. vice
squad so she can spend more time with her daughter. Holden Thomas sees only a
woman with a job that's too dangerous for a mother. So the bachelor guardian
strikes Robbie off his list of mommy candidates for the little girl under his care.
Too bad he can't resist the attractive cop's charms!

#1275 THE RANGER'S SECRET by Rebecca Winters
When Chase Jarvis rescues an injured passenger from a downed helicopter, the
Yosemite ranger is stunned to discover it's the woman he once loved. But he is
no longer the man Annie Bower knew. Will she forgive him for the secret he's
been keeping for ten long years? And will he forgive Annie her own secret—the
daughter Chase didn't know he had...?

#1276 A WEDDING FOR BABY by Laura Marie Altom
Baby Boom
Gabby Craig's pregnancy is a dream come true. Too bad the father is an
unreliable, no-good charmer who's left town. And when his brother, Dane, steps
in to help, Gabby can't help relying on the handsome, *responsible* judge. But
how can she be falling for the brother of her baby's daddy?

www.eHarlequin.com

HARCNMBPA0809